SIAMESE IN THE SUN

Noodles lifted his head, then bounded off the window-sill, his eyes fixed on the goodies in James's cupped hand.

There was a splintering crash, and Ming sprang off Mr. Allardyce's lap in fright. Noodles had blundered straight into the oil lamp, sending it flying to the floor, where the delicate glass shattered.

"Noodles!" Thomas Allardyce said sternly, jumping out of the chair. "Behave yourself!"

Mandy was just reaching out to help James up when a heartrending cry made her freeze. It was a sound not unlike a human baby — a very unhappy human baby. Goose bumps rose on Mandy's arms. She spun around to see a pitiful sight.

"Ming!" Mandy exclaimed. "Oh, *Ming* — what's happened to you?"

Give someone you love a home!
Read about the animals of Animal Ark™

1	Kittens in the Kitchen	21	Raccoons on the Roof
2	Pony on the Porch	22	Dolphin in the Deep
3	Puppies in the Pantry	23	Bears in the Barn
4	Goat in the Garden	24	Foals in the Field
5	Hedgehogs in the Hall	25	Dog at the Door
6	Badger in the Basement	26	Horse in the House
7	Sheepdog in the Snow	27	Pony in a Package
8	Cub in the Cupboard	28	Puppy in a Puddle
9	Piglet in a Playpen	29	Tabby in the Tub
10	Ponies at the Point	30	Pup at the Palace
11	Owl in the Office	31	Mare in the Meadow
12	Lamb in the Laundry	32	Cats at the Campground
13	Kitten in the Cold	33	Hound at the Hospital
14	Goose on the Loose	34	Terrier in the Tinsel
15	Bunnies in the Bathroom	35	Hamster in the Holly
16	Hamster in a Handbasket	36	Husky in a Hut
17	Squirrels in the School	37	Polars on the Path
18	Fox in the Frost	38	Labrador on the Lawn
19	Guinea Pig in the Garage	39	Kitten in the Candy Corn
20	Shetland in the Shed		

Special #1: The Kitten That Won First Prize
and Other Animal Stories

SIAMESE in the SUN

Ben M. Baglio

Illustrations by Ann Baum

**Cover illustration by
Mary Ann Lasher**

AN
APPLE
PAPERBACK

SCHOLASTIC INC.
New York   Toronto   London   Auckland   Sydney
Mexico City   New Delhi   Hong Kong   Buenos Aires

For Mary Tapissier, who has been a good friend
to Animal Ark; her advice and ideas have
always been very much appreciated.

Special thanks to Ingrid Maitland

ISBN 0-439-68757-8

12 11 10 9 8 7 6 5 4   4 5 6 7 8 9/0

Printed in the U.S.A.   40
First Scholastic printing, October 2004

One

"Oh, it's tiny!" cried Mandy Hope, pressing her forehead to the plane's window. "Much smaller than I thought it would be. Look, James."

"Where?" James Hunter, Mandy's best friend, strained against his seat belt to get his first glimpse of the island of Jersey. He and Mandy had been waiting for the aircraft to break through the cottony layer of clouds carpeted below them. Now it had, and James gave a small whoop. "I see it!"

The little island floated in a sun-drenched sea of bright blue. Mandy could see the Atlantic Ocean rushing up long sandy beaches and swirling into coves.

1

Rocky cliffs gave way to fields of neat green farmland between neat seaside towns. It looked like the perfect place for a vacation.

"Mom!" Mandy called across the aisle to her mother. Emily Hope looked up from the book she was reading. "The island is so beautiful!"

"Great, isn't it?" agreed her father, Adam Hope, who had the window seat beside Mandy's mom. "It's only nine miles by five, yet about eighty thousand people live on it."

Dr. Emily rubbed her eyes and began to gather up her stack of papers. "Not long now." She smiled at Mandy. Then, as the plane banked sharply to turn, her hand shot out to steady a large book propped open on her tray table.

"Would you put your tray table in the upright position for landing, please?" a passing flight attendant asked Dr. Emily. Mandy's mom nodded, smiling, and started filing her papers into a leather briefcase at her feet.

Mandy turned back to watch the horizon tilt as the plane swooped lower for landing. She was finding it hard to sit still. She and James had spent the flight looking at pictures of the most unusual cat breeds in the books Dr. Emily had brought with her. Mandy's mom was going to be the official vet at a prestigious annual cat show, and she was using all her spare time to read up on different breeds and ailments. Names like Russian Blue, Foreign White, Balinese and Siamese, Tonkinese and Ragdoll swirled in Mandy's head until she felt as if she knew more about cats than most people.

"Surfers!" James said excitedly. "See, Mandy? It would be great if we could rent some boards." Mandy and James shared great memories of boogie boarding in Cornwall one summer.

"Don't worry, we're going to have time to do and see everything," Mandy replied happily. She quickly scooped her blond hair into a ponytail. This was going to be a vacation with an added bonus: They were going to be staying at a veterinary clinic that would give animal-crazy Mandy a chance to meet some four-legged locals, too!

Mandy's parents were both vets who ran their own busy practice called Animal Ark in Welford, Yorkshire. For one week of the summer vacation, Dr. Emily and Dr. Adam had agreed to take over a veterinary practice in the Jersey village of Beaumont that was run by old friends Colin and Anna MacLeod. Mandy knew that the MacLeods were away in Italy at a veterinary conference and had left their son, Craig, at home to be supervised temporarily by Mandy's parents.

"I wonder what he'll be like," Mandy said aloud, her nose to the window.

"Who?" asked James.

"You know . . . the MacLeods' son. Craig." The only thing she could remember about the boy who'd come to visit nine years ago when she was three years old was that they had found a plump, pink earthworm and played with it in the garden.

James wasn't listening. "Look at those waves!"

"I hope he'll show us around," Mandy continued. "One thing's for sure, he'll be as crazy about animals as we both are, so we'll definitely have something in common."

"Who?" James said again maddeningly, propping his elbow on the armrest as he leaned across Mandy to peer down at the golden stretch of sand below.

"It doesn't matter," Mandy said, and laughed. She clearly wasn't going to be able to compete with the prospect of some seriously good surf, so she gave her full attention to the ground rushing up to meet them. As the plane dipped lower, she spotted a field of emerald green, dotted with golden-brown cows.

"Jerseys!" she exclaimed. "My favorite breed of cow. They have the best faces."

"Another great beach! It must be low tide," James chipped in. "You know, I read that Jersey has one of the highest tidal ranges in the world, up to forty feet."

"Wow," said Mandy, impressed. She gripped the armrests of her seat as the plane gave a sudden sharp lurch and the wheels thudded onto the runway. She strained against her seat belt as the plane braked hard.

"We're here!" she announced, smiling broadly at her father. Dr. Adam gave her a thumbs-up sign from across the aisle of the plane.

They were soon inside the airport terminal, a low concrete building buzzing with people on vacation. Small children milled around clutching bucket and spade sets and inflatable swim toys, calling to one another in high-pitched voices. The scent of suntan lotion wafted in the air. James hurried off to find a luggage cart and helped load it.

"Honestly!" Dr. Adam grumbled playfully, grabbing suitcases as they cruised by on the conveyor belt. "You'd think we were staying a year, not a week!"

"That's mine." Dr. Emily lunged for her own bag and swung it to the floor. "And that's it, Adam."

"Thank goodness for that," Dr. Adam remarked, steadying the teetering pile.

"Look," said James, prodding Mandy to get her attention and pointing. A young woman standing on Mandy's left was pushing a cart holding a pet's carrying case. A fluffy white poodle was crouched inside. The dog's immaculate coat had been groomed to a snowy frizz around its small pointed face, and it wore a little plaid coat. As soon as its owner stopped the cart by the conveyor belt, it began a high-pitched, excited whining.

"There, there, darling Fifi!" The woman bent down and fumbled to open the case. "Did you have a good flight, dolly?"

"I wish I could have brought Blackie along," said James, suddenly looking a bit gloomy.

Mandy linked arms with him. "He'll be a lot happier at home in Welford, chasing rabbits."

"You're right," James said. "But it would have been fun to have him with us."

Mandy tugged James along as her dad set off with the cart. "Besides," she reminded him, "there'll be all sorts of animals to keep us busy at the MacLeod clinic."

Up ahead, Mandy's parents were waving at a young woman who was holding a sign. On it was written THE HOPE FAMILY in bright red letters.

"Over here!" Dr. Adam called. The woman waved back and came over, holding out her hand.

"I'm Jennifer Locke, Colin and Anna's receptionist. I'm glad I found you. Mid-July is the height of our tourist season, and the island is packed — you see the crowds!"

"This is Mandy, our daughter," Dr. Adam told her. "And James Hunter, Mandy's friend."

"Welcome, all of you." Jennifer smiled. "Colin and

Anna are so glad you were able to take time to be here. Come on, let's get out of this mob."

As Jennifer turned to lead them to the parking lot, she almost collided with the bulging red eyes of a huge inflatable dragon. Short bare legs stuck out from underneath it, and a distinct giggle came from behind the dragon's ferocious head.

"Ooops!" Jennifer said, and gasped.

"Sorry," said a harassed-looking man who was standing a short distance away. "Tommy! Come here — now!" The dragon bobbed unsteadily away, still giggling.

Jennifer strode ahead with her hands deep in the pockets of her jeans, her long braid of glossy black hair swinging. As Mandy hurried along behind her, she noticed a poster announcing the island's forthcoming cat show and pointed it out to her mother. Dr. Emily nodded and smiled, but she was too short of breath from carrying her hand luggage to reply.

Jennifer's car was a spacious, rather battered-looking van, with plenty of room for the five of them and their luggage. She steered the van along a road that clung to the coastline, allowing them dramatic views of chalky cliffs carved out by the strong Atlantic tides.

"What a wonderful place," Mandy said.

"Yes, beautiful, isn't it?" Dr. Adam agreed, nodding enthusiastically.

Just then, Mandy spotted a slate sign propped against a boulder on the side of the road: CREAM TEAS. She turned to grin at James.

He patted his tummy. "Hmm, yum," he said.

Jennifer laughed. "There'll be plenty of time for those, I'm sure. This," she continued, "is St. Austin's Bay, our nearest beach. Beaumont is just around the next bend."

As the village came into view, Mandy felt excitement fizz inside her. Pretty terraced houses, brightly painted, shared the beachfront road with a row of shops. As Jennifer eased the van carefully past an ice cream cart that had attracted a crowd of people in swimming suits, Mandy spotted a village shop, a small café, and a bookstore before they turned into the driveway of MacLeod's Veterinary Clinic. It was an old whitewashed building, the top half of which, Jennifer pointed out, was where the MacLeods lived.

As soon as the van stopped, Mandy got out, eager to explore. James heaved his small suitcase out of the trunk, and Mandy's father wrestled with the other bags. Jannifer led them around the building to a side door. Behind the clinic was a yard, and Mandy saw a goalpost at the far end of the lawn.

"Will Craig be here?" she asked.

Jennifer glanced at her watch. "He should be around, though he might be at soccer practice. Let's go inside and see."

Inside, Jennifer led them into a pleasant living room. Mandy was suddenly hopeful that there might be a cat curled in one of the big, soft chairs, but she couldn't see one.

Upstairs, Jennifer directed Mandy's parents to the MacLeods' room, then led Mandy and James to their rooms.

"We hoped you'd be OK here, James," she said, opening the door to a small study lined with bookshelves and with a neat computer table under the window. An inflatable mattress took up most of the floor space, with a sleeping bag on top. "It's the study, really, but we didn't have any other spare rooms," Jennifer added apologetically.

"It's fine, thanks." James looked pleased and Mandy laughed.

"This doesn't mean you can surf the Internet by night as well as waves by day!" she joked.

"Mandy's just across from you," Jennifer went on, stepping across the hall to open another door.

"Oh, it's lovely!" Mandy exclaimed, stepping into a sunny little bedroom that overlooked the bay. She put her suitcase down and went to the window. The waves shone like glass in the midmorning sun. "Thank you, Jennifer," she said.

"It's going to be fun having you here. Now, let's see if Craig is around," she said.

They followed her up yet another flight of stairs to a tiny third-floor landing. Jennifer knocked on the only door Mandy could see. "Craig?" she called softly. "Are you there?"

There was no reply, so Jennifer opened the door. Mandy peered past her shoulder. The walls of the small room were draped in the blue and white colors of a soccer team announced as Kilmarnock on one of the many banners, and there were posters of soccer players everywhere. A dark-haired boy was lying on his back on the bed, reading a magazine.

"Oh! Hi," said Jennifer. "I'm sorry to burst in on you. I thought you were out. I wanted you to meet Mandy and James."

Craig didn't move, not even lifting his head off the pillow to look at the visitors. Mandy shifted uncomfortably and glanced over her shoulder at James. Craig must be really shy!

"Hi," she offered, looking back into the room.

"Nice to meet you," James added, standing on tiptoe to look past Mandy and Jennifer.

Craig looked up and raised his eyebrows at the three of them. Then he went back to his magazine without saying a word.

"Well . . . we'll see you later, I guess," Jennifer said cheerfully. "Sorry to have disturbed you." She turned and smiled at Mandy and James. "OK! That's the tour. Do you two want to unpack, or may I get you something to drink?"

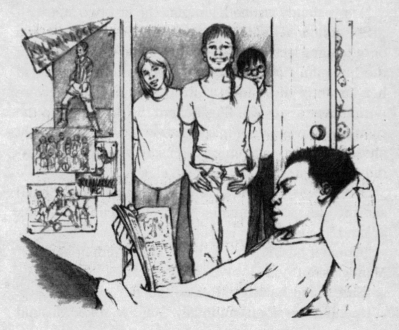

Mandy spoke for them both. "Please, could we see the clinic now?"

"Sure! Are both of you crazy about animals?" she asked, going down the stairs.

"Absolutely," James assured her.

"Crazy," Mandy agreed. "I really hope I'll be a vet one day."

"Well, I can't say I'm surprised," Jennifer said, and chuckled. "After all, with both parents as vets, you must have had a lot to do with animals."

"Yup." Mandy grinned, jumping the last two steps.

She followed Jennifer across the carpeted hall to a door leading to the clinic. The clean, scrubbed smell of the linoleum flooring in the reception area reminded her instantly of home. Dr. Emily and Dr. Adam were poring over a stack of files behind the desk, and to the right of that was a door marked RESIDENTIAL UNIT. Straight ahead were two examining rooms. It was similar in layout to Animal Ark, only a bit smaller.

"I'm going to go and give your mom and dad a hand settling in," said Jennifer. "You two can just look around."

"Would it be OK if we went into the residential unit?" Mandy asked.

"Sure," said Jennifer. "Help yourself."

Opening the door cautiously, Mandy looked around

the large, airy room. There was a row of cages along one wall.

"Oh, look, James, there's a puppy!" She spoke quietly because the pup was asleep.

"Cute!" said James. "It looks like a Labrador." He read the pup's name in neat handwriting on a small chart propped up at the door: ROSCO.

Mandy put a finger in through the bars to stroke one soft, floppy ear. Rosco woke up and yawned, then rolled onto his back, showing off a plump pink tummy and a small stitched scar. He took Mandy's finger in his mouth and began to chew sleepily, wagging his tail.

"Ouch," she said. "Needle-sharp teeth, but you're still a sweetie!" She gently withdrew her hand. "We'll come and spend time with you tomorrow," she promised.

A beautiful silvery lop-eared rabbit named Lucky occupied another of the cages.

"It's a buck rabbit," observed James. "Look how long his teeth are!"

"That's probably why he's here," Mandy said. "Mom or Dad'll have to trim them back a bit, I expect."

"Here's another dog." James bent to peer into one of the lower enclosures. The wire-haired terrier was deeply asleep and hardly stirred when Mandy read out her name.

"Penny," Mandy read. "Hello there."

Penny was sound asleep and didn't stir at the sound of voices. They fussed over a little mongrel named Fudge, with a bandaged leg, who thrust his muzzle through the bars to lick their hands, and then introduced themselves to a plump tabby cat named Alice. Alice had a small shaved area of stitches on one ear, which she kept swiping at with her paw. She seemed grumpy.

"Poor Alice," Mandy said sympathetically.

"Have you met everyone?" Jennifer poked her head around the door of the unit. "Isn't Rosco sweet?"

"Gorgeous," Mandy smiled. "May we help with anything?"

"Thanks, but it's all done for this evening, Mandy. I wouldn't say no to a bit of help tomorrow, though."

"We'd love to," James said, and grinned. "Just call on us anytime."

"What a treat it's going to be having you two here," said Jennifer.

"Well, I'm sure Craig is just as useful to have around," remarked Mandy, trying unsuccessfully to pet Alice.

"Yes, well . . ." Jennifer broke off as Dr. Emily came in.

"You'd better unpack, dear," Mandy's mom suggested. "Dad and I have a patient coming in. We'll have to think about supper pretty soon, too."

"OK," said Mandy, reluctantly turning away from the

animals. "Come on, James, we'd better get organized. Bye for now, Jennifer."

Taking a last look around the unit, Mandy felt a little shiver of pleasure. It was great to be having a working vacation, doing the thing she loved best: being with animals.

Later, when Mandy was alone in her bedroom, she sat at the window looking out at the sea. A yellow moon threw a shimmering pathway across the surface of the waves. There was a soft knock at the door.

"Come in," Mandy said.

James came in, rubbing his tummy. "I'm sure I won't sleep," he complained. "I think I ate too much pasta."

Mandy laughed. "Look how gorgeous it is out there, James," she said. "Listen, can you hear the gulls?"

"Seagulls? At nighttime?" James peered out the window, looking doubtful. "Shouldn't they be asleep?"

"Well," said Mandy, "it sounds like seagulls to me."

There was another distinctive cry, high and plaintive — and quite close.

"Hey! You're right. Sounds like there's one in the yard down there," James commented. He yawned. "Well, I think I'll try to get some sleep. It'll be a busy day tomorrow."

When James had gone, Mandy got into bed and turned

out the light. She didn't feel the least bit homesick, she realized, and wondered if it had something to do with being in a veterinary clinic. It was all very familiar, in spite of being such a distance from Yorkshire. She heard the cry of the gull again. She had to admit it was an odd-sounding birdcall, high-pitched and wailing like a human baby. Mandy thought of the bird swooping and circling over the dark, restless sea, and then she fell asleep.

Two

Early the following morning, Mandy was woken by the telephone ringing at the bottom of the stairs. She lay in her bed, sleepily watching a breeze lift the curtains at her open window.

"I'm in *Jersey!*" she said aloud, suddenly fully awake. She scrambled out of bed and reached for her shorts and T-shirt.

Outside James's bedroom door, she paused. Her mother's voice reached her from the floor below. "Yes, we're making ourselves at home, Anna," she was saying. "It's so beautiful here on the bay, and the weather is perfect."

Mandy was about to knock on the door when it opened. James jumped when he saw Mandy standing there.

"What's the matter?" he said, looking worried.

"Nothing!" she responded. "I was just going to see if you were up."

"It feels like breakfast time to me," said James, adjusting his glasses.

"What happened to all that pasta?" Mandy teased, starting down the stairs. She turned back to James. "Mom's on the phone with Mrs. MacLeod," she added in a whisper.

"Craig?" Dr. Emily said into the receiver. "Yes, he's here. We didn't see much of him last evening, but we were busy finding our way around. Should I get him for you?"

Mandy was halfway down the stairs, and she waved her hands to get her mother's attention. Dr. Emily looked up.

"I'll get him, OK, Mom?" Mandy offered.

"Oh, thanks, dear." Dr. Emily smiled at James, then went back to her conversation with Anna MacLeod.

Mandy shot back up the stairs to the second floor and on up to Craig's bedroom. It was hot up there, under the roof. Mandy tapped lightly on the door.

"Craig?" she called, suddenly feeling shy. "It's Mandy. Your mom's on the phone from Italy."

The door opened abruptly. Craig looked at her. He was wearing a soccer shirt. "Yeah?" he said.

"Phone," Mandy repeated. "For you."

"OK," Craig said, sliding past Mandy. He took the stairs two at a time, landing at the bottom with a big thump.

"He's here, Anna," said Mandy's mom. "I'll say good-bye, then. Have a great time — and say hello to Colin."

Craig took the phone, and Dr. Emily ushered Mandy and James out of the hall and into the kitchen.

Dr. Adam was sitting at the table, leafing through a thick appointment book. There was a steaming mug of tea in front of him.

"It doesn't look too busy," he said, "for a Saturday morning." He looked up. "Oh, hello, you two! James, you look half asleep."

"No, I'm not." James grinned, quickly combing his tousled hair with his fingers. "I'm just hungry."

"Again?" Dr. Emily groaned playfully. "Well, eat all you want. Adam's been to the grocery store to buy eggs and bread, and there's cereal."

"That was Anna on the phone," she went on, pouring tea from a big brown pot.

"Maple Cross Farm . . ." Dr. Adam was reading aloud from the appointment book and not really paying attention.

"A farm?" Mandy was instantly all ears. "Are you going to visit?"

"Just a routine visit — some postoperative stitches due to be removed," her mom explained.

Dr. Adam stopped reading and took a sip of his tea. "Perhaps we'll arrange to go out on Sunday, Emily. That way we can see some of the island."

"Oh, great idea, Dad!" Mandy said. "And we'll be able to see some Jersey cows up close."

Her father smiled. "But you've seen Jersey cows before, Mandy. They won't be any different, you know."

"Oh, yes, they will," Mandy insisted. "Jersey cows in Yorkshire are not the same as Jersey cows on Jersey Island."

Dr. Adam laughed. "I can't argue with that!"

Just then, Craig came into the kitchen and stopped just inside the door. For a second, everyone was silent. Then Dr. Emily spoke.

"Hi, Craig. Would you like some breakfast?"

"No, thanks," he replied. "I'm going to play a game."

"Soccer?" James asked eagerly, his cornflakes crunching as Craig nodded.

"James is crazy about soccer." Mandy looked at Craig and playfully rolled her eyes.

"Good," Craig answered. "So . . . I'll see you, I guess."

"But won't you have a glass of —" Dr. Emily began, but Craig was out the back door and into the yard before she could finish her sentence. Mandy looked at James. He was staring after Craig, looking disappointed.

"An eager sportsman," Dr. Adam decided, going back to the appointment book.

"I suppose it's not surprising if he's shy," Mandy said. "It can't be easy, having a whole family suddenly arrive in your home."

"Still," said James, glumly, "I would have gone along with him, if he'd asked."

"Yes," Dr. Emily agreed. "That would have been nice. Another time, perhaps, James."

"Doesn't he help around here?" James added. "I mean, with the animals?" He nodded in the direction of the clinic on the other side of the kitchen wall.

"I guess not." Dr. Emily shrugged. "Colin and Anna didn't promise us his help, so we can't really expect him to pitch in."

"He must earn his allowance in other ways," said Dr. Adam, but Mandy thought her father looked as surprised by Craig's offhand manner as she was.

Dr. Emily stood up. "Well, I'm going to go into the

clinic now. Mandy, I'm sure you and James would like to help."

Mandy stood up, sloshing milk from the jug she was holding. "Of course!" She grinned, reaching for an apple with her free hand. "Ready, willing, and more than able!"

"Good." Her mom smiled. "You can start by feeding the animals in the residential unit — but eat something first!"

"I will," Mandy answered, sinking her teeth into the crunchy apple. She was already at the door, with James hard on her heels.

"Let's go!" he said.

Rosco was playing a game with a rubber toy when Mandy and James approached. The puppy's ears shot up happily when he spotted them, and he began to scrabble at the bars with both front paws. Mandy slipped the bolt and lifted him into her arms. The pup licked her face, his tail wagging furiously.

"You're adorable," Mandy told him, smoothing the pale gold fur on his forehead. Rosco tried to chew on her fingers. She put him on the floor, and he tumbled about.

"He's so naughty," James said, and laughed. "Let's distract him with breakfast."

"Good idea," Mandy said. "I'll get it."

Rosco pounced on James's shoelaces and tugged at them, making fierce little growling sounds, while Mandy measured out his morning ration from the recommendation on a little chart hanging on the door. The pup's shiny black nose twitched when he smelled food, and he bounced over to the bowl she set down.

Mandy petted him. "We'd better clean out his cage while he's eating," she said.

"I'll get started on Penny." James nodded toward the scruffy little terrier in the cage adjoining Rosco's. The dog still seemed sleepy, but she perked up when James came close, then began to tremble nervously.

"Don't worry," James said soothingly, petting the top of her head. "The scary part is over, girl. I'm here to make you more comfortable." He'd helped Mandy in the residential unit of Animal Ark before. Now he was almost as practiced as she was at the routine chores.

Mandy smiled as she stripped Rosco's bedding. He came waddling over to lie curled against Mandy's foot and gave a contented sigh.

"How's it going?" asked Dr. Emily, coming into the room. She was wearing a white coat that seemed a little too big.

"Fine," Mandy answered. "Are you and Dad finding your way around?"

"With Jennifer's help, yes," she said. "It's a well-organized place. We shouldn't have any problems." She looked at her watch. "We have a poodle coming in soon."

"What's up?" Mandy asked.

"The owner said she has a piece of bone embedded in her gum, poor girl," Mandy's mom replied as she opened a drawer neatly labeled SURGICAL GLOVES.

"Can Mandy and I take Rosco into the yard?" James asked.

"You can — but not today, James. We don't want him undoing all the good those stitches are doing him," said Dr. Emily, looping a stethoscope around her neck. "Now I have to go and scrub up. How about having a walk around the village when you're finished in here? We could use some more milk."

"Sure," Mandy said, dropping a kiss onto Rosco's soft yellow muzzle. "We'll go off and explore as soon as we've finished."

Mandy's mom smiled. "Thanks, both of you. You're great assistants, you really are."

When Lucky, Penny, Fudge, and Rosco had been fed and were back in their cleaned cages, Mandy and James slipped out through the reception area and onto the street. Mandy waved to Jennifer, who was talking on the phone.

"Too bad we don't have our bikes," James remarked, squinting in the sunlight.

"It's a tiny place!" Mandy said. "We can walk. And," she added, "we won't have Blackie tugging us furiously along after some smell he's picked up."

James smiled. "You're right," he said.

The village of Beaumont was filled with Saturday shoppers. Mandy and James walked to the left, out of the clinic's parking lot, and a few paces along, Mandy stopped.

"Gibb's Groceries!" she said, her hands on her hips, gazing at the sign. "It's right next door to the clinic — so Dad didn't have to go far at all this morning."

"Let's go the other way," James suggested. "We can pick up milk on the way back."

"OK," said Mandy.

As they walked along the busy main street, Mandy hoped they would find a turn that would take them to the beach. She could hear the gulls; it couldn't be more than a few minutes' walk. They went on down the street, past small glass-fronted shops and a row of blue-and-white-painted houses. One side of the road opened onto a rectangle of smoothly cut grass, with a gray stone

church on the other side. As they drew closer, they
could hear a chorus of enthusiastic yelling coming from
people standing at the edge of the field. Several boys in
striped soccer shirts were running around in the center
of the field.

"There's Craig!" James pointed. "See?"

"Oh, yes," said Mandy, shading her eyes from the
glare of the sun.

James watched eagerly as the ball was smacked into
the goal. Excited cheers erupted from the spectators.
Mandy saw Craig dart forward and leap for the ball as it
was thrown back onto the field from the net.

"Come on," Mandy said, and tugged at his sleeve.
"He'll invite you to play soon, I'm sure. Let's cross over
now and head back."

"I don't know," James remarked, catching up with
Mandy as she reached the opposite pavement. "Craig
doesn't seem very friendly to me."

"He's just shy," Mandy answered.

They strolled past a toy store, a beauty parlor, a drug-
store, and the bookshop they'd seen the day before,
ending up across from the clinic. Then Mandy spotted a
display of elegant, highly polished furniture in the window next to Gibb's Groceries. "Let's cross back," she
urged James. "I want to look in the window of that
store."

"Allardyce Antiques," James read from a beautifully engraved wooden sign above the door.

"Oh, wow! Just *look* at that ornament," Mandy cried, tugging James onto the sidewalk.

Just inside the window was a wide, flat area raised to the level of the windowsill and carpeted in green felt. There were a number of items laid out for display on it — a decorative glass lamp and an old-fashioned chair with a pretty blue cushion — but Mandy's eyes had been drawn to a delicate porcelain statuette of a cat, curled up tightly with its eyes closed. The beautiful piece had been placed in an obliging spotlight of warm morning sunshine, and its smooth china fur seemed to gleam as though it had been lighted from within.

"It's a perfect model of a Siamese cat," Mandy said admiringly. "Look at the dark points on its ears. I wonder how much it is?"

"I doubt you could afford it," James warned her. "It looks like an expensive shop to me, but it *is* a nice cat," he added.

"Let's go in," Mandy decided. "We'll ask. I'd love to have a closer look at it, anyway."

"OK." James shrugged. "I could lend you some of my pocket money if you want."

"Thanks," Mandy said, reaching for the door handle.

In spite of the sunlight streaming in through the windows on either side of the door, the little shop seemed dark. Mandy blinked a couple of times to adjust her eyes and looked around. It was an Aladdin's cave of treasures, from tiny silver pocket watches to tall wardrobes and ancient chests. Copper kettles and old pots hung from hooks on the walls.

"Now this is the sort of antique I like," James said approvingly, reaching out for a sword in a heavy-looking brass sheath.

"Better not," Mandy warned, edging carefully around a grandfather clock. She stood on tiptoe and craned her neck in the direction of the cat in the window. "There doesn't seem to be anybody here. Do you think it's even open?"

"I hope so," said James.

Just then Mandy gave a gasp of surprise.

James looked around sharply. "What?"

"It's gone!" Mandy cried. "James, look — the china cat is gone and — look!"

The beautiful cat had vanished. In its place, in the exact spot where it had been lying just seconds before, there was a rather large shaggy dog.

Three

Mandy and James stared. The dog scratched lazily at one ear, then shook its head and yawned. Tangled gray-and-white fur hung over its eyes, and its pink tongue dripped steadily onto the green lining of the display shelf.

"But how . . . ?" James began, then stopped, frowning.

Surprised as Mandy was, she couldn't help admiring the dog. It was beautiful! It seemed to be smiling as the warmth of the sun spread through its thick, streaky coat. Mandy felt an urge to spring forward and give it a great big hug.

"Maybe he's sitting on the cat," James suggested.

"That wouldn't be very comfortable," Mandy pointed out. "More likely he's knocked it to the floor. I hope it isn't broken! Let's go over and say hello. Then we'll see."

They made their way carefully around a low, carved table holding a fine porcelain bowl.

"Do you think this dog is friendly?" James asked in a low voice. "It might be a guard dog or something."

"I'm sure it's friendly." Mandy smiled. "Look how sweet its face is! It's snoozing, that's all."

"May I help you?"

James and Mandy jumped, startled. Mandy spun around to see a small, round-faced man standing at the back of the shop. His cheery, interested expression put her instantly at ease. He held a pair of reading glasses in one hand.

"Are you looking for anything in particular?" he added politely.

"Hello," said Mandy. "We were looking at your dog, actually, and also —"

"Ah, Noodles!" The man interrupted her, shaking his head fondly as he came toward them. "He's a character, isn't he? That little spot on the display ledge there, that's his favorite place. It gets the morning sun, you know."

"A perfect place for sunbathing," Mandy said.

Noodles peered up at the man through his bangs. He seemed unwilling to move an inch, though Mandy could see a little stub of a tail twitching in welcome.

"He's gorgeous," she said, reaching over the chair to pat the dog. "Hello, Noodles."

"He's not mine, you know," the shop owner said unexpectedly. "He belongs to the woman next door. He just visits — perhaps a little more often than is polite," he added. "I'm Thomas Allardyce, by the way."

"I'm James Hunter," James told him. "This is Mandy Hope. Her parents are vets, and they're looking after the MacLeod Clinic for a week."

"Ah, yes! Welcome. You'll have a fine time here on Jersey. Glorious weather, isn't it?"

"Yes," Mandy agreed. She couldn't hold back a moment longer from the question she was burning to ask. "Um, Mr. Allardyce, when we were outside your shop we saw an absolutely gorgeous china cat in the window. I'm sorry to have to tell you but . . . it seems to have disappeared! It was right there in the window, and I just hope it hasn't been broken by Noodles."

"China cat?" Mr. Allardyce looked puzzled. "A china cat, you say?"

"Yes," Mandy said with certainty.

At that moment, a shrill little sound rang out from the

back of the shop. Mandy was instantly reminded of the seagulls crying outside her window the night before. To her surprise, Mr. Allardyce burst into laughter.

"A china cat!" he repeated. "My dear, no. I think you must be referring to my beloved and beautiful Ming."

"Ming?" Mandy echoed, confused.

Mr. Allardyce made a sound at the back of his throat. Instantly, a high-stepping Siamese cat with fur the color of pearl emerged from behind a walnut cabinet and padded sedately toward them. Mandy watched, enchanted, as she wove her way delicately through the thin legs of a set of chairs, then arched her back and gave a delicate meow at Mr. Allardyce's feet.

Mandy's hand flew to her mouth. "Oh, wow!" she cried. "You're not made of china — you're real!"

The cat regarded them coolly through her brilliant blue eyes. They looked to Mandy as though they had been circled with a charcoal-colored crayon.

"She is rather beautiful," Mr. Allardyce agreed. "Her full name is Sud Su Ming, which means 'the ghost of a tiger' in Thai. I call her Ming for short."

"How *lovely*!" Mandy bent down to scratch Ming's smooth back, and the cat sank gracefully to the carpet and lay on her side, purring. "Ghost of a tiger!"

"There's not much of the tiger about her, though," Mr.

Allardyce went on. "Noodles will insist on stealing her favorite spot in the window, and Ming is always gracious enough to let him help himself. I think she knows he's lonely, poor fellow."

"Lonely?" asked James. "Why?" He reached down and tickled Ming under the chin. Noodles blinked at them from the windowsill. He was not going to give up the spot he had snatched from Ming, though Mandy guessed he must be roasting in the sun in his furry coat.

"Oh, his owner, Mrs. Gibb, is a busy woman," Mr. Allardyce explained. "She owns the grocery store next door."

"My dad has already been a customer there," Mandy told him.

Ming tipped up her chin and stared at Noodles, who was puffing like a steam train. The cat's fur was as sleek as satin, her ears a deep mink color. Each of her four paws was dark chocolate, fading to fudge brown and then the palest cream. Mandy, who knew enough about Siamese to know they made friends only when they were ready, had to resist an urge to pick her up and hold her close.

"Does Ming go out at night?" she asked.

Mr. Allardyce nodded. "She's as free as a bird. Loves

to wander a bit after dark, but she's usually in her basket when I get up in the morning. Why?"

"Well," Mandy explained, "last night when we arrived, I heard a calling sound that I thought might be seagulls. Now that I've heard her, I think it must have been Ming."

"That's very likely." Mr. Allardyce smiled. "Siamese cats have a very unusual meow, and they can sound just like seagulls. Some people say they sound like babies crying, too!"

"I like your pictures," James said suddenly. Mandy saw that his attention had wandered to the wall of the shop where Mr. Allardyce had hung lots of different framed photographs, paintings, and drawing of cats. James moved in closer to inspect them. "They're fantastic," he said.

"Thank you." Mr. Allardyce sounded pleased. "They're not for sale. I'm crazy about cats, you see, and I like collecting them for my own enjoyment."

"They're great!" Mandy followed James over to the wall and admired the impressive collection of cat portraits. They ranged from pencil sketches of domestic pets to a spectacular white tiger caught on camera in a snowy wilderness. Some were paintings, done in bright oils; others were photographs, yellowing with age.

There was even a collection of comical cat cartoons. As she stood gazing up at the display, Mandy felt Ming swirl silkily, briefly, about her bare legs. She smiled, flattered that the adorable Siamese had chosen her for this show of affection, and she bent to rub the cat's head.

Straightening up, Mandy noticed a black-and-white photograph of a woman smiling proudly, holding a small parasol above her head. She wore a long skirt and beside her was the biggest domestic cat Mandy had ever seen. A trophy cup sat next to the cat on a table.

"Gosh, *that's* an amazing cat," Mandy said. The animal looked directly at the camera, its nose lifted haughtily.

"That's a Maine Coon cat," Mr. Allardyce told her. "They're a fascinating breed. He was a champion of his class in his day, many years ago. Victorian times, that is."

With a graceful spring, Ming landed on the padded armrest of a nearby chair and began a soft, contented purring. Mandy was enchanted. She cupped Ming's perfect little face in her hands, admiring the striking contrast in color between her head and her body. Examining her closely, it seemed to Mandy that Ming looked different from other Siamese cats; she had the familiar blue eyes and chocolate points, yet her face was rounder and softer looking than the more triangular Siamese cats she'd seen at Animal Ark.

James reached out to pet Ming. "She's so beautiful," he said. Then his face lit up as if he'd had a really good idea. "Mandy's mom is going to be the vet on duty at a big cat show here on Friday. You could enter Ming. I'm sure she'd win."

Mr. Allardyce sat down on a wicker chair, and Ming sprang onto his lap and settled herself comfortably. Her owner ran his hand over her sleek back.

"Well," he said, laughing, "it's very nice of you to say so, but, you know, it isn't quite as straightforward as simply entering her."

"What do you mean?" Mandy asked.

"Ming is an Applehead Siamese and, gorgeous though she is, I don't believe she has much of a chance competing against these modern Siamese cats."

"I noticed that she looks a bit different," Mandy admitted.

"Yes," Mr. Allardyce confirmed. "Cat breeding is subject to fashion, like everything else, and for the last few years judges and breeders have favored a sharper, more exotic look in the breed. Wedgeheads, they're called," he added.

"Oh," said Mandy, disappointed. "But that doesn't mean they're prettier or more well-bred than Ming, does it?"

"*I* don't think so, my dear." Mr. Allardyce smiled at her. "But there's more to a prize than just being pretty, isn't there? I mean, fashion has to be considered as well."

"I don't understand," said James, wrinkling his nose. "What's a Wedgehead? It sounds like something you'd use to prop open a door."

Mandy and Mr. Allardyce laughed.

"The standards of the show ring are constantly changing," Mr. Allardyce told them. "Breeders these days seem to favor Wedgeheads because they are exotic and sleeker, with larger ears and much sharper features. My Ming is rounder in appearance, as you see, rather robust, with a nice round, dark face."

Ming looked up and narrowed her eyes at them. Then she gave a little toss of her head and began licking her front paw. Mandy thought it was as though she were saying, "I don't care what the standards for show cats are — I like the way I look!"

"Besides," Mr. Allardyce went on, "I think I've got enough on my hands with the shop to run and Ming to care for — and my pesky visitor over there." He wagged a fond finger in Noodles's direction. The dog was still basking, though the sun had moved slightly, and he seemed unaware that he was the topic of conversation.

"He's cute," James stated, adding rather proudly, "I have a dog. He's a Labrador named Blackie."

"A Labrador!" Thomas Allardyce looked interested. "I'll bet he's full of energy, like Noodles."

"Yes, he is," James agreed, going over to Noodles's perch to offer him some attention. "He's lots of fun. I really like dogs — and cats, of course."

Out of habit, James put his hand into the pocket of his jeans and groped around for the treats he usually carried for Blackie. Mandy watched him pull out a few dog biscuits, broken into bits after the long trip from Welford. At once, Noodles lifted his head, then bounded off the windowsill, his eyes fixed on the goodies in James's cupped hand.

There was a splintering crash, and Ming sprang off Mr. Allardyce's lap in fright. Noodles had blundered straight into the oil lamp, sending it flying to the floor, where the delicate blue glass shattered. James lost his footing as the dog collided with his legs. He fell in a heap on the floor, and the crushed biscuits flew into the air. Splintered glass lay everywhere.

"James!" Mandy cried. "Are you all right?"

"Noodles!" Thomas Allardyce said sternly, jumping out of the chair. "Behave yourself!"

Mandy was just reaching out to help James up when

a heartrending cry made her freeze. It was a sound not unlike a human baby — a very unhappy human baby. Goose bumps rose on Mandy's arms. She spun around to see a pitiful sight.

"Ming!" Mandy exclaimed. "Oh, *Ming* — what happened to you?"

Four

Ming was behaving very strangely — so strangely that, for a moment, nobody moved. Watching the little cat tossing her head about and writhing on the carpet at first made Mandy think she was having some kind of a fit.

Her heart turned over, and she and Mr. Allardyce reached out for the Siamese at the same moment.

"Ming!" Mandy cried. "Oh, Mr. Allardyce, what is it?" Mandy tried to hold the distressed little creature, but she squirmed out of her grasp. Thomas Allardyce put a soothing hand on his cat's back, trying to calm her.

He withdrew his fingers quickly and put them to his

41

nose. "Oil!" he said, frowning. "It's oil from that broken lamp. It's all over her, poor girl."

"Oil?" James repeated. He had his hand looped through Noodles's collar and was struggling to hold the dog, who was still sniffing about furiously in search of biscuit crumbs. The table that Noodles had crashed into had a cracked leg, and there were splinters of glass everywhere. The brass base of the old-fashioned lamp lay on its side; the last drops of oil trickled onto the floor and soaked into the carpet.

Ming yowled, using first one paw, then the other to wipe her face.

"I think she's got oil in her eyes," Mandy said urgently. "Quick! Let's take her next door to the clinic."

"Good idea," Mr. Allardyce scooped the oily little cat into his arms and hurried off after Mandy, who shot ahead through the maze of furniture to the door and held it open. James let go of Noodles and charged after them.

Jennifer Locke looked up in surprise when the three of them burst through the reception door. Ming's crying alerted a small dog waiting to be seen, and it began a frantic yapping. An elderly man with a budgie in a cage at his feet covered his ears and scowled at the noise.

"Mandy!" said Jennifer. "What on earth has happened?"

"Is my mom with a patient, Jennifer?" Mandy asked. "Is my dad free? Ming's covered in lamp oil, and it's gotten into her eyes. She needs help."

The front door opened behind them, and Mandy hoped that it wasn't another emergency patient, or Ming might have to wait. She turned and with relief saw that it was only Craig who had come in.

"Your father is out in the residential unit," Jennifer said to Mandy. "I'll get him right away." She said hello to Craig as she slipped past him.

"Craig —" Mandy began, but she didn't finish her sentence. The door to the waiting area suddenly flew open, and Noodles scrambled in, his paws slipping on the linoleum floor. He made straight for James, who was standing close to Thomas Allardyce, petting Ming.

"Hello, Noodles!" said James.

"Craig," Mandy began again, trying unsuccessfully to grab hold of Noodles's collar and clean up at the same time. "Can you help us? We need an extra hand to —"

"I can't," said Craig, moving quickly through the chaos toward the door to the stairs leading to the apartment. "I'm going back out in a minute. Sorry."

"Oh . . . OK," said Mandy.

Noodles was leaping around all over James. His shaggy bangs bounced, and his bright eyes looked merry and mischievous. *"Sit!"* Mandy commanded, but Noodles took no notice.

"No more treats," James said sternly. He showed the dog his empty hand. "See? All gone."

"In here, Mr. Allardyce," Jennifer called, opening the door to one of the examining rooms. "Dr. Adam will see Ming right away."

Thomas Allardyce looked red-faced and he was out of breath as he struggled to hold Ming in his arms. She fought him, twisting and turning and rubbing her face against his sweater. She cried out again and again, and the sound pierced Mandy's heart as she followed Mr. Allardyce into the examining room. What if Ming had tiny fragments of glass in her eyes?

Dr. Adam immediately held out his arms to the distressed Siamese. Mr. Allardyce seemed glad to hand her over.

"Thank you," he said, flustered. "Will you be able to get rid of the oil?"

"Oil?" Dr. Adam asked, looking puzzled.

"Dad, this is Mr. Allardyce from the antique shop. A lamp broke in the shop, and the cat was splashed." Mandy explained it as simply and efficiently as she could.

"Good to meet you, Mr. Allardyce," said Dr. Adam, his eyes never leaving Ming. "Poor girl," he soothed. "Keep still now, and let me have a look at you."

Ming sat miserably on the stainless steel tabletop, her little body shuddering with fear. She tried to lick at the oil on her forelegs, then coughed and spat.

Dr. Adam widened her eyes and looked into them with a flashlight. "I can't see any damage," he said. "But she does have oil in her eyes — kerosene, is it?"

"Yes, yes." Thomas Allardyce nodded, looking anxious. "A silly accident."

Mandy helped her father hold Ming on the table. Outside in the waiting room, she could hear James having stern words with Noodles. Then she remembered that in their hurry to get Ming to the clinic, they'd left the door to the antique shop wide open!

"Mr. Allardyce," she said quietly, "would you like me to close up your shop for you?"

"The shop?" he said absently. "Oh! *The shop* — goodness, I've left the door open. I'd better go back, the lock's a bit tricky. May I leave Ming here with you? She'll be OK now, won't she?"

"Of course," Mandy assured him. "We'll look after her, don't worry."

"Thank you so much," said Mr. Allardyce, making hurriedly for the door.

A moment later, James appeared in the examining room. "He's gone," he announced. "The dog, I mean. Noodles. He trotted out after Mr. Allardyce. How's Ming?"

Dr. Adam was just easing an injection into the cat's upper back leg. "I'm going to give her a sedative," he said. "She's very upset; this will calm her."

"Dad, is she going to be all right?" Mandy asked, her fingers caressing the only bit of fur she could find that had no oil on it. She watched as the sedative took effect and Ming sank slowly onto the table. Her chocolate-colored head dropped onto her front paw, and she closed her eyes.

Dr. Adam looked serious. "Kerosene can be absorbed through the skin," he explained. "It *can* be very nasty because it can damage the liver, and in some cases, that's fatal. But thanks to your prompt action, we've caught this in time."

"What are you going to do?" asked James, his eyes as wide as saucers.

"I'm going to start by flushing out her eyes with sterile water," Mandy's dad replied, moving around the room and gathering supplies. "Then we'll wash her very thoroughly and apply a substance that will dissolve the oil from her fur."

"Poor Ming." Mandy sighed. "Cats hate water."

"She's feeling pretty dopey," her father reminded her. "She won't be scared. James, could you fill the basin at the sink with warm water for me, please? About half-way up."

"Sure," said James.

Once Ming's eyes had been washed, James brought over the basin of water, and Dr. Adam lowered the cat gently into it. Mandy held her head while her father went to work massaging the cat with a strange green jelly.

"Yuck," said James, holding his nose. "What a smell."

"I agree." Dr. Adam laughed. "But it does the trick."

To Mandy's relief, Ming seemed unconcerned as the smelly paste was rubbed deep into her fur. James stood at the ready with a bucket of clean water and poured it carefully over her back at intervals, while Dr. Adam rinsed her again and again.

When it was over, Ming looked very bedraggled and sorry for herself, but her coat was completely clean. Dr. Adam wrapped her in a towel and handed her to Mandy. "She's starting to come around now. Rub her dry. Then you can take her back to Mr. Allardyce," he said. "She doesn't need to stay in the residential unit. She's close enough for us to keep an eye on her for the next couple of days."

"OK. Thanks, Dad." Mandy cradled the Siamese in her arms. She lay back like a baby, still sleepy and confused, her small face hooded in the towel. Then she opened her eyes and blinked rapidly a few times. Mandy gently stroked her with the towel to dry her off.

"Will you give Mr. Allardyce these eyedrops?" Dr. Adam asked. "They are protective anti-inflammatory drops. He should use them twice a day." He handed a small bottle to James.

"Right," James said, reading the label.

When Ming's sleek coat was smooth and shiny once more, they set off for Allardyce Antiques.

Jennifer was back behind the reception desk, working at her computer. She looked up as they went past. "How is she?" she asked.

"Fine now." Mandy grinned. Ming's beautiful eyes were wide open, and she snuggled in closer to Mandy.

"Hey! What's this?" James said suddenly, pointing to the floor.

Mandy looked down. A thin trail of blood, scuffed by dog footprints, stained the linoleum.

"Oh!" Mandy said. "Was the little dog that was in here earlier bleeding?"

"No," said Jennifer, coming around from her desk to look at the floor. "He came in for an injection."

Mandy and James stared at each other in dismay, both clearly thinking the same thing.

"Noodles!" James cried. "It must be Noodles. That glass . . ."

"And we never noticed!" Mandy berated herself. "Poor Noodles!" She felt a stab of guilt. She'd been so worried about Ming, she hadn't thought to check if the big, bumbling dog had been injured, too.

"Quick, Mandy," said James, flinging open the door and making Ming meow in surprise. "Let's go and see if he's hurt!"

They found Thomas Allardyce in his small kitchen at the back of the shop. It was chaotically untidy, the limited countertop space crowded with papers and the small wooden table still holding the remains of Mr. Allardyce's toast and marmalade. Mandy put Ming down. She immediately jumped onto a chair and began grooming herself meticulously.

"Oh, good job!" said Mr. Allardyce when he saw Ming's clean coat. "Thank you both so much." He gathered her up lovingly, and she began to purr in his arms. "She's as good as new!"

"Mr. Allardyce, is Noodles with you?" asked James, looking around anxiously.

"I expect so," he said. "Yes, there he is. Over there —

for some reason the silly dog has squeezed himself right under that chair."

"We think he's hurt," Mandy told him. "There's blood on the floor of the clinic."

"Oh, dear," said Mr. Allardyce, frowning.

James and Mandy went over to where Noodles was lying under a low padded chair, licking repeatedly at an upturned front paw.

"It's cut, all right," James said grimly. "It looks sore."

"Oh, poor Noodles!" Mandy squatted to peer under the armchair.

Noodles wouldn't let Mandy touch his paw, but she could see that it would need stitches. The glass had sliced quite deeply into the soft, rounded part of the pad.

"This is all my fault," said James. "If I hadn't offered Noodles a treat, none of this would have happened."

"Don't blame yourself," Mandy told him. "It was an accident, that's all."

James nodded gloomily, and Thomas Allardyce put a kind hand on his shoulder.

"Just bad luck, boy," he said. "Look, would you two be kind and take Noodles to the clinic to have his paw looked at? I'll see if I can get hold of Mrs. Gibb, his owner. She ought to know."

"Yes, of course, Mr. Allardyce," Mandy said.

"Thank you both so much," he replied. Looking at his cat, he smiled gratefully.

Ming lay contentedly in his arms now, looking around her with interest, like a queen on a throne.

"Come on," said Mandy. "Let's get patient number two next door!"

It was late in the afternoon by the time Noodles's small operation was over. Dr. Adam and Dr. Emily had been busy, and because the dog's cut paw hadn't been considered urgent, Mandy and James had to wait. Noodles seemed subdued as he sat in the waiting room. James held him tightly on a leash that he'd found in the residential unit, but Noodles was too busy licking his sore foot to be any trouble. Around one o'clock, Jennifer brought in a plate of sandwiches for Mandy and James, and Noodles showed only mild interest. His nose twitched and he sniffed loudly but didn't get up to investigate the source of the delicious smell. Finally, he emerged from the examining room with four neat stitches and a solid bandage around his leg.

"Noodles!" James crouched down and hugged the dog. "I'm sorry, boy."

"The stitches will dissolve in time, Mandy. Will you tell that to Mrs. Gibb, please? She won't have to bring him back to have them removed."

"OK, Dad," Mandy replied, smoothing Noodles's shaggy head with the palm of her hand. "Good boy," she told him, and clipped a leash to his collar.

James and Mandy walked him slowly, gingerly back to Gibb's groceries. A sign in the window read CLOSED, so they went next door to Mr. Allardyce's shop. Opening the door, Mandy saw he had a customer, a middle-aged woman with blond hair.

"Ah! Here he is now!" Mr. Allardyce had spotted them at the door.

"Noodles!" The woman hurried over and stooped to give the dog a cuddle. "What have you been up to now?"

"Sarah Jane," Thomas Allardyce said, "this is Mandy and James, the two youngsters I was telling you about. Mrs. Gibb has just come back from a trip to the other side of the island, so she's just heard about the accident."

"Hello," James and Mandy said together.

"Thank you, thank you," Mrs. Gibb said gratefully. "You've been a wonderful help."

"Well," James began, looking guilty, "I haven't been really . . ." Mandy stopped him with a nudge.

"We're glad to have helped," she said, and smiled.

"There was a small piece of glass in Noodles's paw," James reported. "Dr. Adam dug it out, and he's going to be fine. He has a few stitches."

"Dissolving ones," Mandy added. "You won't have to bring him back, my dad said."

"I'm very grateful," said Mrs. Gibb. She pushed back the dog's thick bangs with her hand and looked into his eyes. "What am I going to do with you?" she asked, and sighed.

"To be honest, Sarah Jane," Thomas Allardyce spoke

up, "he's becoming a bit of a nuisance in the shop. He's just too boisterous to be jumping around in here! It's not the damage to the lamp or anything that I'm worried about, but I'd hate to see him get hurt again."

"I know." Mrs. Gibb shook her head sadly. "I think it's because he's bored. He loves to get out, but really, I don't have time to walk him."

"Could we help?" Mandy offered automatically. She was sure they'd be able to fit a little dog-sitting around their chores in the clinic.

"Yes!" James sounded very enthusiastic. Mandy guessed he wanted to make amends for the accident.

"Well," Sarah Jane hesitated, "that would be very kind. Noodles would love to get out a bit more. He hasn't had many really good long walks since my son left for the university on the mainland."

There was a tap at the door, and Emily and Adam Hope came in. Mandy made the introductions.

"Clinic's closed for the day," Dr. Adam said. "We just came by to check on these two."

All eyes turned to Ming and Noodles. Ming was making her way delicately across the floor to the spot in the window she loved. She paused to lick at a patch of damp coat, then jumped up and glared pointedly at her rival, who was still sitting by Mrs. Gibb. Noodles was watching her with his head cocked to one side and his ears pricked. For a second, it looked to Mandy as though the dog was going to challenge Ming for the best sun-bathing spot. He started forward, then seemed to think better of it. He lifted his sore leg and looked at James with a mournful expression on his face. Then he sighed and lay down instead, his head on James's foot. Ming curled up in the window for a nap.

"Ming has reclaimed her territory!" Mandy declared. "Good for her. I guess getting oil on her fur was the last straw!"

Five

Midmorning on Sunday, they all drove out to the Sullivans' farm, listed in the appointment book. It had dawned cool and cloudy after an overnight rain, but Mandy thought it made the island look even more beautiful. The sea seemed restless; it was pearly gray rather than blue, and the low clouds only made the strong summer colors below more intense.

Mandy sat in the back of the MacLeods' Land Rover looking eagerly around her. Outside Beaumont, the trees lining the narrow roads met overhead, making a tunnel of soft green light.

"Do you think Mrs. Sullivan will mind us coming along?" she asked her father.

"I don't think so," he replied, adding teasingly, "unless you intend to kidnap one of her calves!"

Mandy laughed and passed James a roll of peppermints.

"I like the way cows *smell*," James remarked, his cheek bulging with the mint. "They remind me of how a meadow smells."

On Mandy's side, a field of buttercups spread down to the sea. A group of young heifers looked up from their grazing to stare curiously as the Land Rover passed. It was such a gorgeous place! Mandy wondered what it would be like to live on the island all the time, and that made her think about Craig.

"What's Craig doing today?" she asked out loud.

Dr. Emily turned and held out her hand for a mint. "I'm not sure, but he seemed happy enough to stay behind. Soccer has been canceled because of the rain. The field is wet, he told me."

"He should have come along with us!" James said generously.

"Yes," Mandy agreed.

"I offered," said Dr. Emily. "He didn't seem very interested."

"He's still feeling shy," Mandy concluded. "It's a shame."

"He must feel awkward, having us in his home," said Dr. Adam. "He's just a private sort of person, I think."

"I know," said James, "we could ask him if he wants to walk Noodles with us later."

Dr. Emily smiled at him. "That's a good idea. But don't take it personally if he says no. If he wants to get involved with us, he'll let us know."

Mandy sighed. "It's a shame," she said again. She couldn't understand Craig. The long summer vacation stretched before him — and all the wonderful animals that came and went from his parents' clinic. Yet he didn't seem a bit excited about any of that.

"Look, James," said Dr. Emily, pointing. "Another place serving cream teas!"

"Oh, yum!" James rubbed his tummy dramatically.

"Honestly," Mandy teased, holding the peppermints away from James's reaching hand, "at this rate you're going to explode before we get back to Welford!"

"Here we are," said Dr. Adam. "Misty Hills Farm."

A white fence surrounded a few acres of lush green pastures at the side of the road.

"Gosh," Mandy said. "It looks lovely."

Dr. Adam pulled into the gravel driveway and drove slowly toward the big house. In the center of a circular parking area, there was a small island of plants. The noise from the engine startled a skinny light brown cat who shot out from under a bush and leaped up the nearest tree.

"That," said Dr. Emily, getting out of the car and pointing in the direction of the vanishing cat, "is a Cornish Rex."

"Oh, great, Mom!" Mandy said approvingly. "You can spot these breeds at a hundred feet after all the reading you've done."

"I don't want to be stumped by any technical questions from the breeders at the show," her mother replied, giving her a wry smile.

"Good morning!" A woman in Wellington boots was striding toward them. "You must be Colin's replacements. I'm Aline Sullivan. Thanks for coming."

Dr. Emily and Dr. Adam shook her hand and introduced James and Mandy.

"You must be very interested," Mrs. Sullivan said, smiling, "to come out to a farm on a Sunday morning just to see some stitches being taken out."

"We are," Mandy replied. "We'd love to see the animals, if you don't mind."

"I don't mind a bit." She turned to Mandy's parents. "Would you take a look at one of my calves while you're here?"

"Gladly," said Dr. Adam, lifting his big black veterinary bag.

"We enjoyed the drive here," said Dr. Emily, falling into step beside the farmer. "We haven't had much time to drive around."

"Well, I won't keep you too long from exploring further," said Mrs. Sullivan. "This way!"

They followed the farmer to the milking barn. Treading carefully in the ooze of mud along the path, Mandy spotted a large herd of pale brown cows in the adjacent pasture. They pulled at the grass, flicking their tails to keep the flies away. One or two of the more curious animals ambled up to the fence.

"Aren't you pretty!" Mandy said.

Beside her, James was breathing in deeply. She tweaked his T-shirt.

"I told you," James grumbled. "I like the smell!"

Mandy feasted her eyes on the animals' beautiful faces. Huge liquid brown eyes gazed at her with interest, and they blinked long lashes and lifted their wet gray noses to sniff at her hands.

Mrs. Sullivan took them to a calving pen. Three calves lay dozing in the straw. When Mrs. Sullivan led the Hopes in, two of them clambered to their feet in alarm. The tiniest calf remained where it was.

"This is our little Katie," explained Mrs. Sullivan,

crouching down beside her. "She was born small, five weeks ago. She's not been eating much recently...." She trailed off, looking up at the Hopes.

James and Mandy squeezed up to the railing. Mandy wanted to be as close to the little calf as possible without getting in the way. Katie stared at them with big, bewildered eyes. Then she stood up nervously on her wobbly legs. Mandy wanted to reach out to her, but she knew better. The calf was sick, she could see that. Katie was struggling to breathe, and her nose was running.

"My bet is that she has a respiratory infection," Dr. Adam said right away, delving into his black bag for a thermometer. "I'll just take her temperature."

The calf skittered away from Dr. Adam as he approached. Mrs. Sullivan slipped her arms around Katie's neck, holding her still and talking to her in a soothing tone.

"Yes, her temperature is up," Dr. Adam said after a moment. "I'll give her an antibiotic injection and also an anti-inflammatory shot. That should clear things up."

"She'll be much better soon," Dr. Emily assured the farmer. "But give us a call if she doesn't start eating normally within the next couple of days."

Mandy watched her father as he filled his syringe and inserted the needle quickly into the big muscle on the calf's back, near her tail. Katie shifted, alarmed, but it was all over in seconds.

"Poor Katie," Mandy said quietly.

"It's a fairly common infection in calves," her mother told her. "We've caught it in time, so it won't turn into pneumonia. That's the main thing."

"Good," said James, stretching an arm through the railing to risk a gentle pat. Katie didn't move, so Mandy put out her hand and touched her velvety ear.

"Oh, she's amazing," she whispered.

"I expect you've worked up an appetite," Aline Sullivan

said, opening the gate of the pen. "I hope so, because we use our own dairy cream to make the most scrumptious cream teas."

"Wow!" James's eyebrows shot up. "Really? Here?"

"Right here, up at the back of the house. Would you like a scone?"

"Oh, yes," James said, and grinned.

"Sounds good to me," agreed Dr. Emily.

"Excellent," Dr. Adam joined in. "I'll join you after I've removed those stitches."

"Ah, yes, that'll be Doris. She's outside in the field. I'll take you to her," Mrs. Sullivan said.

"Don't eat all the scones, James!" Dr. Adam warned. "I'll be back in a few minutes."

Mandy laughed as she went out into the yard, squinting in the bright sunshine.

Dr. Emily caught up with her. "Well," she said, "*are* they any different from the Jersey cows we have at home?"

"Yes," Mandy insisted. "I think they are. Somehow, they seem to belong here — much more than they do out on the moors."

Dr. Emily slipped an arm around Mandy's shoulders and gave her a quick hug. "And now we're about to sample Jersey cream from Jersey cows on Jersey," she said. "What could be better?"

*   *   *

James would have agreed. Ten minutes later, when they had washed their hands in the kitchen, Mrs. Sullivan served them all the promised cream tea. Dr. Adam carried the tray to a wooden table outside, and James sprang up to help unload a plate piled high with delicious-looking scones. There was a pot of strawberry jam and a bowl brimming with thick, yellowish cream.

"Mmmm," said Dr. Emily. "What a bonus! Thank you."

Mandy poured juice for herself and James; for the adults, there was tea. James sliced his fluffy scone in two and slathered it thickly with cream first, then added a generous dollop of jam.

"Fantastic," he said, smiling at Mrs. Sullivan.

"I'm glad you like it," she answered.

When neither James nor Mandy could eat another mouthful, they asked if they could go have a look around the farm. Mrs. Sullivan readily agreed and refilled the teacups for Dr. Emily and Dr. Adam.

They walked to the field where the Jersey herd was grazing. Mandy climbed astride the split-pole fence. The sun had come out, and several cows lay basking, chewing their cuds.

A few of the smaller, younger cows were walking toward the fence. As they came nearer, the nervous little heifers drew up short of the barrier, stretching their necks to investigate the hands of the strangers from a safe distance. By keeping very still, Mandy attracted a curious calf who came close enough to snuffle the palm of her hand.

All too soon, Mandy heard her mother calling.

"Time to go!" Dr. Emily waved at them from the other side of the field. When Mandy jumped down from the fence, the cows scattered in all directions.

Walking back toward the Land Rover, James spotted the cat Dr. Emily had identified as a Cornish Rex. It had found an upturned milk crate to sit on and was grooming itself with its eyes closed.

"Only a few more days till the show," Mandy remembered. "It's going to be such fun."

"Yes," James agreed. "It's a shame that Ming won't be taking part, though, especially now that her coat is so clean!"

Then, as Dr. Adam dangled the car keys loudly to urge them to hurry, he and Mandy broke into a run.

When they arrived at the clinic, Craig was in the backyard kicking a soccer ball around. He raised a hand in silent greeting, then went back to aiming at the goal.

James bent down by the back door to take off his muddy sneakers. Suddenly, the side gate opened, and Noodles burst in and fell upon James with glee.

"Noodles!" cried Mrs. Gibb, who was dragged in behind her dog. "*Stop* it!" She tugged hard at his leash. "I was just coming to ask if you'd mind giving him a walk before lunch, Mandy?" she added as James hopped around trying to retrieve one of his shoes.

"Yes, we'd love to." She smiled, trying hard not to laugh at poor James. Noodles obviously adored him.

"Oh, good," Mrs. Gibb said. "How kind of you."

She closed the side gate behind her and unclipped the dog's leash. Noodles bounded around; every bit of him seemed to be trembling with excitement. Suddenly, he spotted the ball — and Craig. He went lumbering over, his large pink tongue lolling.

For a moment, Mandy hoped the friendly dog might encourage Craig to join them on a walk. But it had the opposite effect. She stared in amazement as Craig snatched up his soccer ball and tucked it firmly under one arm. Then, giving Noodles a wide berth, he marched briskly across the lawn and, his eyes fixed on the ground, slipped in through the side door of the house. The door closed with a slam behind him.

Six

There was no time to wonder about Craig's bad mood. Noodles quickly turned his attention to Mandy. He ran over, jumped up, and put his two big front paws on her shoulders, barking joyfully.

"He's such a handful," said Sarah Jane Gibb, shushing the dog with a wave of her hand and giving Mandy the leash. "Do you think you can manage?"

Mandy grinned as she eased Noodles down to the ground. "Oh, we're used to dogs who are a handful," she said.

James was barefoot, brushing off the dirt from the

farm that had gotten between his toes. "He can't be bouncier than Blackie!" he agreed, grimacing.

"You'd better put your shoes back on," Mandy told him. "Noodles is ready to go right now."

As James pushed his feet into his sneakers, Dr. Emily rapped on the kitchen window to attract their attention.

"Would you two like something to drink?" she asked, opening it and looking out at them.

"We're going to take Noodles for a walk," Mandy explained. "Is that OK?"

"Fine," she said. "See you later. Have fun."

Mandy had secured Noodles with a short leash. Now she handed it to James. "You can take him first, since he likes you so much!" She smiled.

James was immediately tugged in the direction of the gate to the yard. Noodles seemed to know exactly where he was going.

Mandy caught up with them, laughing. "It's just like being at home with Blackie," she said.

The sky had been washed to a beautiful blue by the rain. Mandy had a spring in her step as she walked briskly beside James, who was trying to keep Noodles in check. The dog coughed, and James hurriedly slackened the leash. They'd turned left out of the clinic's parking lot and headed along the main street. Mandy spotted Mr. Allardyce outside his shop, and she waved.

"I wish I could let Noodles off the leash," said James. "He'd like a good run, in spite of his sore leg."

"He's only limping slightly," Mandy said. "And if this walk goes well, maybe Mrs. Gibb will let us take Noodles to the beach tomorrow."

Noodles, it seemed, was well known around Beaumont. Several people reached out to pat him on the head as they passed, and some asked about his bandaged paw. One woman with dark curly hair stopped to offer him a dog biscuit from the basket she was carrying.

"I know you," she said, stopping and rubbing the dog on the head, "but I don't know who *you* are!" She smiled at Mandy and James.

Mandy smiled back. "I'm Mandy Hope, and this is my friend James Hunter. We're staying at the MacLeods' veterinary clinic."

"We offered to take Noodles for a walk," James explained.

"Sarah Jane will be pleased!" said the woman. "Is his paw healing?" Mandy and James had squeezed to the side of the narrow sidewalk to allow people to pass. But Noodles was impatient to get going and kept pulling on the leash and coughing loudly. They were attracting quite a few looks.

"Yes." Mandy laughed. "It doesn't seem to have slowed him down one bit!"

"Oh, dear," the woman said. "We're making nuisances of ourselves. Look, I'll tell you what. I have a big yard with lots of lawn. Would you like to bring Noodles along for a change of scene? I understand he might not be able to run in the park until his paw is better."

"Well . . ." Mandy began hesitantly.

"I'm Deborah Stewart," the woman introduced herself. "I know the MacLeods and Sarah Jane Gibb — and I only live a few doors down, at number eighteen." She pointed along the street.

"OK, thank you," Mandy said.

Mrs. Stewart stepped briskly ahead, her basket swinging. Mandy and James followed.

While they walked the short distance to number eighteen, Mandy explained to Mrs. Stewart that both her parents were vets.

"Ah," she said. "I know something about your mother! Isn't she going to be the on-site vet at the cat show here on Saturday?"

"Yes," Mandy said, feeling rather proud. Her mother was famous already!

"The whole village is looking forward to the show," Mrs. Stewart continued. "We have visitors coming from all over the world — even as far as Japan!"

"Wow," James said as Mandy felt a small pang of excitement.

"Here we are," said Mrs. Stewart, fishing in her basket for a key in front of a whitewashed cottage with a slate roof.

Mandy guessed that she was a devoted gardener because there were earthenware pots brimming with exotic flowering plants everywhere. She looked around her nervously. "Are you sure Noodles is safe in your garden? I'd hate it if he broke anything."

"He'll be fine," said Mrs. Stewart, leading them indoors. "All he wants is space to tear around and let off a bit of steam. Here we are, James." She opened a glass door to a lovely yard. "Let him rip! I'll get you both a cold drink. You look as if you deserve one!"

Noodles was giving off little yelps of joy as James undid the clasp and let him go. His paws scrabbled against the polished floorboards in his eagerness to explore. He shot out the door and tore off across a smooth green lawn surrounded by a blaze of colorful flowers.

Mandy and James watched him for a moment, then Mandy went into the kitchen to help Mrs. Stewart. On the way through the living room, she noticed a cat curled up in a smooth little ball in the center of a deep, puffy cushion. One chocolate paw lay loosely over its face, and a gentle rumble came from the cat as it snoozed.

Mandy stopped. "A Siamese!" she said aloud, just as Mrs. Stewart appeared with a tray.

"Do you like cats?" She smiled. "I adore them. This one is my pride and joy, Supreme Champion Black Forest Gateau."

Mandy gaped at the cat, then at Mrs. Stewart. "Is that really his name?"

"Yes," she answered, setting down the tray on a coffee table in front of the sofa. "Just Gateau for short. It means 'cake' in French, you know. Very fitting — he's chocolate in color and certainly sweet enough!"

Mandy laughed and pointed out the sleeping cat to James as he joined them.

"Oh, wow," he said, his hands on his hips. "Another one!"

"You have a Siamese, do you?" Mrs. Stewart looked very interested. She paused as she was pouring cola into two glasses.

"No," James shook his head. "I don't. But we met one."

"Ming," Mandy explained. "She belongs to Mr. Allardyce."

"Ah, Ming!" Deborah Stewart smiled. "Yes, I know Thomas's lovely Ming quite well. She's an Applehead Siamese, like Gateau."

As though he knew he was being talked about, the cat slowly uncurled and opened first one eye, then the other. He stretched lazily, then jumped off the sofa and ran across to his owner, calling out a noisy greeting.

Mrs. Stewart gathered the cat into her arms and kissed his face before setting him down in her lap. Settling against her, Gateau put out a languid front paw and gently batted at the earring dangling from Mrs. Stewart's ear.

"Oh, no, you don't, you mischievous old man," she chided him, laughing. "He's full of tricks, in spite of his age."

Gateau soaked up the attentions of the two visitors, purring as they stroked and petted him. His magnificent chocolate paws kneaded the soft wool of his owner's lilac sweater.

"He *looks* like a champion!" Mandy said, admiring the almost black face of the cat.

"Oh, yes," said Mrs. Stewart. "He's a champ all right. He's won the Gold Challenge Certificate three times. He's retired now, of course."

"Did he like it?" asked James.

"Being shown?" Mrs. Stewart was tickling her cat under his chin. "He loved the attention he got," she replied. "As I'm sure you know, Siamese are very sociable animals and make wonderful pets. They're affectionate, fun, and highly intelligent — not to mention gorgeous to look at!"

Gateau raised his chin, looking his most imperious, and everybody laughed.

"Cat shows have an important role to play," Mrs. Stewart went on. "Careful selection of the very finest cats helps keep the breed strong because the cats pass on those strengths to future generations."

"I think the Appleheads are beautiful!" Mandy declared. "But Mr. Allardyce told us that they aren't as popular at shows now."

"Well, Appleheads are one of the oldest breeds of domestic cat in the world. They look much the same as when the breed was originally imported from Siam — a muscular, athletic cat with a round head and brilliant blue eyes." Mandy noticed a fleeting shadow of sadness crossed Deborah Stewart's face. "I hope they don't die out altogether as a breed."

Mandy was thinking about this when she heard James splutter and gasp. She looked across at him, surprised. His face was a picture of shock. He was kneeling at the foot of Mrs. Stewart's armchair, staring straight ahead, his fingers frozen in Gateau's soft fur. For a moment, Mandy thought he might be choking — he seemed unable to speak — then a sudden movement made her look down at James's bare legs. A large, brightly colored snake had entwined itself around his left thigh.

"Oh!" said Mandy, startled.

Just then, the door flew open, and a tall, dark-haired young woman rushed into the room.

"Mom, have you seen Kellogg?" she said, sounding exasperated. "I've looked — oh, hello, sorry to interrupt."

"Kellogg?" James squeaked.

"Is Kellogg a snake, by any chance?" Mandy asked.

"That would be my Kellogg," the girl said cheerfully.

"Right . . . there." Mandy pointed slowly, wondering if any sudden movement in James's direction might alarm the creature.

"Oh, *there* you are!" said the girl, striding toward James.

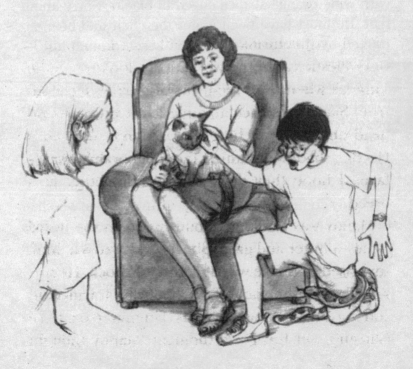

"Does he bite?" James wanted to know, in a very small voice.

Mrs. Stewart peered down at the snake in surprise. "Goodness, Kellogg! The places you turn up! He's a harmless little fellow, James, even if he should have been called Houdini! Nicole, this is Mandy and James. They're staying at the MacLeods', and Mandy's mom's going to be the vet at the show."

"Hi!" Nicole responded, stooping to unwind the snake from James's leg. It was more than two feet long, with wide orange stripes edged in black. "Sorry about that. He must have been under the chair and been attracted by the warmth he could sense around him — and that was you!"

"Oh," said James, relief spreading across his face as the snake was uncoiled and removed. "I was just surprised."

"I'm sure you were!" Nicole laughed, her dark brown curls jiggling. "Don't worry about Kellogg. He's a corn snake. I've had him for ages, and he's a great friend."

Mandy couldn't help feeling sorry for James, who had turned very pale. He took a sip of his cola just as Noodles began scraping loudly and persistently at the door from outside.

"May I let him in?" asked James, glancing at Kellogg.

"I'll take Kellogg to his vivarium," said Nicole. "He's

not interested in food at the moment, and I'm trying to encourage him to eat."

James hurried to let Noodles in. The dog was panting from his run around the garden. His stumped tail wagged hard as he went around the room greeting everybody in turn. Then, to Mandy and James's surprise, he flopped down at James's feet and gave a big sigh of contentment.

"That run certainly did him a lot of good," Mrs. Stewart commented. "It's lovely to see Noodles behaving calmly. You must be a good influence, you two!"

Nicole had draped Kellogg around her neck like a scarf, and the snake seemed happy. His head bobbed about, and Mandy watched, fascinated, as he suddenly disappeared down the back of Nicole's T-shirt.

"How was work this morning?" her mother asked her.

Nicole made a face. "We're so busy!" she said, wriggling her shoulders as Kellogg reappeared at her neck. "We're expecting this huge crowd of visitors to be staying at the hotel because of the cat show, and there's so much to do to get ready."

"Nicole works at the Bay Hotel," Mrs. Stewart explained, stroking Gateau. To Mandy's amazement, the elderly Siamese looked completely untroubled by the appearance of the snake and the dog.

"I'm still trying to think up an idea for a theme for the weekend, something that will unite all the cat lovers,"

Nicole filled them in. "I thought it would make a nice welcome."

"Is there going to be a celebration dinner or something?" Mandy asked, interested.

"No, more like a display in the lobby of the hotel. I don't know . . . I just haven't settled on anything suitable yet." Nicole sighed. "Perhaps it's not such a good idea after all."

"You don't have much time left to get it done," Mrs. Stewart reminded her.

Nicole groaned. "Don't I know it!"

Kellogg wrapped gently around his owner's face as she spoke, and James began to giggle. Only the lower half of the girl's face was visible. She looked to Mandy as though she were wearing an exotic hat.

"Enough!" Nicole said, and laughed, standing up. "I think Kellogg is trying to tell me something. He might even be hungry at last, with any luck. It was nice to meet you both."

"Bye," Mandy said. "Good luck finding your theme for the hotel."

"Thanks."

Gateau stood up and stretched luxuriously in Mrs. Stewart's lap. Mandy thought again how beautiful he was. "Mrs. Stewart," she asked, "do you think there will be any Applehead Siamese entered in this year's show?"

Now that she'd met these two glorious specimens, she was eager to see some more.

"I'm not certain, Mandy," replied Mrs. Stewart. "I don't know anybody who has registered an Applehead for entry around here."

"What about Gateau?" James suggested.

"He's way past it now, I'm afraid," Mrs. Stewart said.

"Well, what about Ming?" Mandy piped up.

"Ming?" Mrs. Stewart raised her eyebrows. "Well, Ming, of course, is a beauty, but Thomas Allardyce won't enter her. At least, I don't think he will."

"Do you think she has a chance of winning?" Mandy persisted.

"I think so, yes." Mrs. Stewart nodded. "It would be wonderful, but knowing Thomas as I do, I really don't think he'd be interested."

Mandy stood up. "I think people should be reminded how Siamese cats used to look. Wedgeheads are beautiful, but Appleheads deserve equal recognition."

Mrs. Stewart smiled. "I'm sure Thomas would agree with you, but . . ." She raised her hands, palms up, and shrugged.

"Let's go and talk to him," said James. "I'll bet he'll listen to us."

"It's time we went back, anyway," Mandy said. "Thanks for having us, Mrs. Stewart."

"It's been so nice to meet you," she said. "And to see Noodles quiet for a change!"

Noodles stood up obediently, and James clipped on his leash. At once, the dog began to tug James gently toward the door as though he expected another adventure.

"What time is it?" Mandy asked James as they waved good-bye to Mrs. Stewart.

James grinned. "Mr. Allardyce's shop is still open, if that's what you mean!"

"Right," said Mandy. "Come on! We have some persuading to do!"

Seven

They found Mr. Allardyce polishing a copper vase. When the door opened, he looked up and removed his glasses.

"Hello there." He smiled. Standing, he put out a hand to keep a bouncing Noodles at bay. "No you don't, my friend."

James tugged a little harder to keep the dog in check.

"Hello, Mr. Allardyce," Mandy said. "How's Ming?"

"Almost as good as new!" he replied. "She went out for a prowl last evening as if nothing had happened."

"Good!" Mandy and James said together.

Mr. Allardyce glanced at his wristwatch. "I was just

thinking of closing up. Is there something I can do for you?" he said kindly. "Or have you come to visit Ming?"

Mandy smiled. "Well, we wanted to *talk* to you about Ming. Are you in a hurry to leave?"

"Never in a hurry to leave the company of good friends," said Mr. Allardyce, his eyes twinkling. "Pull up a chair, both of you. This sounds like business to me."

"May I let Noodles wander?" James asked. "He's been running around all morning, so I think he's feeling less boisterous."

"In that case, yes. He'll probably go and find poor Ming — but we're used to that!"

Mandy couldn't wait to tell Mr. Allardyce about the idea that had been simmering in her mind ever since she'd spoken to Mrs. Stewart. She clasped her hands on her knees and looked seriously at him.

"We have come to ask you if you would enter Ming in the cat show on Saturday," she began. "You see, we think she might enjoy it, and other people would love to see her, I'm sure."

"How kind you are to think of her!" Mr. Allardyce smiled, looking every inch like a proud father. "But you see, it's not that I'm not in *favor* of cat shows, it's just that it would mean closing my shop for a whole day. Also, she'll need grooming and —"

"We could groom her!" James put in.

"I could take care of the shop for you!" Mandy added.

"No," James shook his head. "That wouldn't work. You have to be at the show to help your mom, remember?"

"Oh, yes," Mandy said with a frown.

"May I ask *why* you're so eager for Ming to compete?" asked Mr. Allardyce, looking from Mandy to James and back again.

"She's so beautiful!" Mandy blurted out. "She would perfectly represent the breed — her breed — at an important show. After all, Appleheads are an ancient, traditional breed."

"That's right," said James. "It's really important."

"Sounds like you've been having a chat with the experts!" Mr. Allardyce chuckled.

"We've been talking to Mrs. Stewart," Mandy confessed. "She told us that she used to show Gateau, but he's too old now. She thought Ming would be a great candidate."

"But do you really think she has much of a chance against the Wedgeheads?" Mr. Allardyce wondered.

"Yes!" Mandy said with determination. "Anyway, the main thing isn't winning but showing people there are other, more traditional types of Siamese. We don't need a judge to tell us that Ming is the most beautiful cat on the island!"

"Well." Mr. Allardyce was silent for a moment, thinking. Then he slapped his hand on his knee in triumph. "I have an idea. Why don't *you* enter her in the show? I'll entrust Ming to your good care. You can prepare her for the show and enter her yourselves. You'll still have time to help your mom. How about that?"

"Really?" Mandy's eyes were wide. "That would be great!"

"We'll make you proud," James promised. "She'll be the best-looking cat there."

Thomas Allardyce laughed. "Well, then, that's settled. Just tell me what you need to do to enter her."

"Thanks, Mr. Allardyce." Mandy jumped up. "I'll check with Mom and let you know."

James went over to get Noodles, who had discovered a few remaining crumbs from the dog treats James had spilled and was enthusiastically licking the carpet.

"Come on, boy," he said. "We'd better get you back to Mrs. Gibb." He clipped on Noodles's leash once more.

"Good-bye for now," Mandy said to Mr. Allardyce. "We'll let you know what needs to be done."

"Good," said Mr. Allardyce, patting Noodles. "After all, there isn't much time now, is there?" And to Mandy's delight, he looked almost as excited as she was about the prospect of entering Ming in the show.

Mandy had hoped to have her mother's full attention

when they reached the clinic, but as soon as they entered the waiting room, she knew she was going to be disappointed. Nicole Stewart had just arrived with Kellogg in a cloth bag. She looked worried.

"A corn snake!" Mandy's mother was saying as Mandy and James put their heads around the open door to one of the examining rooms. Kellogg raised his head and blinked at her, swaying lightly from side to side. "Isn't he handsome?"

"Isn't he?" Nicole agreed, smiling a greeting at James and Mandy. "But he hasn't had an appetite, so I thought I had better bring him in. I'm sorry to come on a Sunday, but I am really worried."

"It's no problem. We were only going to have a sandwich for lunch, so it can wait. Let's take a look at you," Dr. Emily said, gently lifting the snake out of the bag. James stood well back from the table while Kellogg's eyes were examined, and Mandy guessed he was still feeling wary after his dramatic introduction to the snake.

"His eyes are cloudy, which means he's about to shed his beautiful skin," said Dr. Emily, "but I can't see any mites in either eye, so that's good." She ran her hand slowly down the length of the snake's body, feeling for any swellings. Then she opened Kellogg's mouth by pressing softly on either side of his jaw. Mandy watched, fascinated. They very rarely treated reptiles in Welford, and she knew she'd have to learn lots about them when she studied to be a vet.

Shining a small flashlight inside the gaping pink cavity, Dr. Emily saw what she needed to make a diagnosis. "Oh, I see what the problem is," she said. "His tongue is pale rather than a healthy red. I think he has an infection in his mouth. Infectious stomatis, it's called."

"Gosh," Mandy said. "That sounds serious."

"Can it be treated?" Nicole asked anxiously.

"Very simply," said Dr. Emily. "I'll give you some antibiotic drops. It should clear up quite quickly. Then he'll get his appetite back!"

"Thank you." Nicole smiled gratefully. She opened the cloth bag, and Kellogg slithered into it, eagerly seeking the familiar dark. "Poor Kellogg. I'm not surprised he hasn't wanted to eat if his mouth's been sore."

Mandy and James followed Nicole out to the waiting room while Dr. Emily went to the storeroom to get the drops. Jennifer smiled at them briefly, then went back to her computer. She had come into work to catch up on some ordering while the clinic was officially closed.

"Have you come up with any ideas yet? For your hotel theme, I mean?" James asked Nicole.

The young woman shook her head. "No, I'm still hoping for inspiration," she admitted.

"Here we are." Dr. Emily held out a small bottle, but

as Nicole reached to take it, Kellogg's bag slipped from her grasp. The snake fell to the floor with a dull thud.

"Kellogg!" Nicole gasped as her pet poked his head out of the opening and began gliding rapidly toward the cover of the reception desk. At that moment, Craig came into the room.

"Grab him!" Mandy yelled, lunging for Kellogg before he vanished under the desk. The corn snake slithered out of reach.

James got down on his knees beside Nicole, while Dr. Emily dashed around to the other side of the desk in an attempt to head Kellogg back out into the open. Mandy glanced up at Craig, and she was so surprised by the expression on his face that, for a second, she couldn't move.

Craig had turned chalk white. His eyes bulged and his mouth hung open. His back was pressed up against the door to the hall, his fingers splayed against the white wood behind him. Without taking his eyes from the floor, he tried to take a step backward, then realized the door was shut. Mandy saw that he was breathing very fast. He shut his eyes tight for a second, then opened them and sprinted across the room and out the front door to the street. It was all over in a second — and nobody except Mandy seemed to have noticed!

Dr. Emily gave a triumphant cry. "Got you!"

Mandy turned her attention back to Kellogg and watched as the last inches of his marked tail disappeared back into the bag, expertly guided by Dr. Emily.

Nicole held the bag tightly with both hands. "Phew!" she said. "Sorry about that! Thanks so much for your help. I'd better get him home right away."

"He'll be fine," Dr. Emily said reassuringly as Nicole headed for the door. "Just don't let him get out on the main street!"

When Nicole had gone, Dr. Emily gave a big sigh. "What a day!" she said, firmly latching the front door. "I need a cup of tea." She turned to Mandy. "Was that Craig I glimpsed dashing through here?"

"Yes," Mandy said. "But then he headed straight out again."

"Well, I'm sure he'll come back when he's hungry," said Dr. Emily. "I'm going to have lunch, and then there are piles of paperwork to sort out. Coming?"

The first chance Mandy had to talk with her parents about Ming was over supper that evening. They were gathered around the kitchen table, eating a delicious stir-fry. Craig had not appeared, and when Dr. Adam suggested that Mandy might like to knock on his door, she declined.

"No, Dad," she said pleadingly, not relishing the task.

"I really think he just wants to be left alone. He hasn't spent a minute with us since we got here."

"He must be hungry," Dr. Adam pointed out. "I think he ought to eat something."

"I'll take him up a tray a bit later," said Dr. Emily, passing James another helping of salad. "Let's leave him in peace."

Mandy didn't want to think about Craig. She was curious and a little bit worried about his odd behavior, but she was determined he was not going to spoil their excitement over entering Ming in the show.

"Mr. Allardyce has said that James and I can enter Ming in the show!" she reported happily, changing the subject.

"The gorgeous Siamese who came into the clinic yesterday?" asked Dr. Emily. "Well, I think she has as good a chance as any."

"Do you?" James asked eagerly. "Do you really? Only, you see, Appleheads are not so popular these days. Judges favor the more modern-looking Wedgehead Siamese who are . . ."

"Slow down!" Dr. Emily held up a hand, laughing. "James, you sound as if you have been studying the breed books I brought with me!"

"But it's true," Mandy said sadly. "Mrs. Stewart and Mr. Allardyce told us that modern Siamese are all the rage now, and the traditional shape and color of the Appleheads are appearing less and less often in shows."

"So we really want to enter Ming," James went on. "It's not fair that the Wedgehead Siamese are getting all the attention.

"I absolutely agree," said Dr. Emily. "Let Ming stand up for her breed at the show."

"Great!" Mandy cried. "What do we have to do before the show?"

"Do?" said Dr. Adam. "Not much — except let Mom check that her eyes are clear and bright again. That's all there is to it."

"Brush her, obviously," Dr. Emily mused. "And generally make sure she's in the best possible condition. I'll give the show secretary a call in the morning. We'll have to fill out an entry form for Ming."

"Oh, I can't wait!" Mandy stood up. "May James and I have a look at your cat manuals? I want to know everything there is to know."

"Of course," Dr. Emily replied. "*After* you've washed the dishes," she added, her eyes sparkling.

Mandy found the pile of manuals on show cats in her parents' room. She sat cross-legged on the carpet at the foot of the bed, and she and James began leafing through one on showing cats.

"Exemption, Sanction, and Championship," he read, his glasses slipping down his nose in the warm summer night air. "Sounds confusing."

"We need to read up about championships," Mandy said knowledgeably. "That's the one we're interested in. You see, it says here that —"

The shrill ringing of the phone on the bedside table interrupted her. Mandy got up to answer it. "Hello?"

"Is that Mandy by any chance?" asked a faint voice.

"Yes," she said. "This is Mandy Hope."

"Hello, Mandy, this is Anna MacLeod. I'm calling from Italy. Is your mother there, or your dad?"

"Um, I'm afraid my mom's in the bath," Mandy said. "And Dad has gone out on a call."

"Oh, well, it doesn't matter, really. I just wondered how Craig was doing."

Mandy froze, her thoughts racing. Should she let Craig's mother know about his strange behavior? She didn't want to tell tales, but he did seem to be unhappy, and Mandy was worried about him.

"I don't think he's doing well at all," she blurted out. On the floor, James turned sharply to look at her, and his eyebrows shot up.

"What?" said Mrs. MacLeod. "Why? He's not ill, is he?"

"No," Mandy hesitated, unsure of what she should

say. James had covered his face with both hands and was shaking his head as if to warn her to say nothing.

"Maybe I shouldn't say anything, Mrs. MacLeod," Mandy went on, "but he seems really unhappy. I'd like to be his friend, but he doesn't seem to want to have anything to do with me . . . us," she finished, turning away from James, who had pretended to faint in dismay. He was lying flat on the carpet.

"Oh, poor Mandy," Anna MacLeod said sympathetically. Her voice sounded small and very far away. "You must be confused! I'm sorry Craig is being antisocial. It has taken him a while to adjust to having to leave Scotland and his friends and school. He never wanted to move to Jersey, you see."

"Oh," said Mandy. "I didn't know that. We were in the clinic today, with Nicole Stewart's pet snake, Kellogg, and Craig came in and then he charged through the waiting room and out the front door as though . . ."

"Snake?" Mrs. MacLeod repeated, speaking over Mandy. "Did you say snake?"

"Yes, Kellogg. He's a corn snake."

"Oh, dear, Craig is petrified of snakes!" his mother exclaimed. "When he was little, he went away to a summer camp and was bitten by an adder. He had to be rushed to a hospital, and he never got over the shock."

"Gosh, how awful!" Mandy said. "Was he hurt?"

"I think it stung, but he responded quickly to treatment," Anna MacLeod explained. "He was just very frightened; he was only five at the time," she continued. "I sometimes think it was then that he decided not to have anything further to do with animals. He tries to avoid them as much as he can, which isn't easy with vets for parents."

Mandy felt a pang of sympathy for Craig. She couldn't imagine living in a veterinary practice and not liking animals! That must be why he didn't help out with any of the chores.

James began waving his arms about to distract her. When she turned, she saw her father standing in the doorway, his eyebrows raised inquiringly.

"Who is it?" he whispered.

"Oh, Mrs. MacLeod?" Mandy said. "My dad's here now. I'll pass the phone to him. Bye."

"Bye, Mandy — and thanks for being concerned about Craig. I'm sure he'll be fine, but seeing that snake today would have given him a shock, that's for sure!"

Mandy gave her dad the telephone, then motioned to James to follow her out of the room.

"Why did you have to tell her about Craig being so moody?" James groaned. "You shouldn't have said anything. He'll be so mad at us!"

"No, it was really helpful. Mrs. MacLeod told me he's scared of snakes," Mandy said. "Apparently, he's found it hard to move here after being in Scotland, so I guess the last thing he wanted was for his mom and dad to go away without him — and seeing Kellogg must have been the last straw!" She led the way to the kitchen.

The lights were out, and Mandy had to grope along the wall looking for the switch. As soon as they were on, James made a beeline for a big tin on the table.

"I feel sorry for him," Mandy continued.

"Me, too," James agreed, his hand in the cookie tin. "But what more can we do to show him we want to be friends?"

Mandy was about to answer when a noise behind her made her turn around. Craig had appeared at the door. He frowned when he saw them. "Oh, hi," he said.

"Hi," Mandy and James said together.

Craig was in his bathrobe, his dark hair wet from the shower. He walked over to the fridge and opened it, looking for something.

"Do you want to come on a walk with Noodles tomorrow?" James asked him. "We might go to the beach."

Craig straightened up, a pint of milk in his hand. "No, thanks," he replied without turning round.

Mandy suddenly felt hot with a mix of concern and annoyance. They were only trying to be friendly!

"Are you still worried about seeing the snake?" she asked.

Craig spun around and stared at her, horrified. "What do you mean? Why should I be worried?"

"Well . . . I . . ." Mandy stammered. She couldn't tell Craig that she had spoken to his mother about him.

James sat down at the table and examined his cookie closely.

"Look, it's none of your business, all right?" snapped Craig, pouring milk into a glass so quickly it spilled.

"But it is," Mandy persisted bravely. "It is my business — because we'd like to be friends!"

Craig put the glass of milk on the counter. "Well, you can start by leaving me alone," he growled. "Just because you love animals doesn't mean everyone has to. Not everyone is like you! So stop interfering, OK? Just stop interfering!" And with that he stormed to the door and stamped up the stairs.

"Oh, no," said James. "Now look what you've done."

Mandy sat down beside him and propped her chin in her hands. "Yes," she said sadly. "I've really ruined things now, haven't I?"

Eight

On Monday morning, Mandy got up as soon as she heard her mother moving around. There was the comforting clink of the teapot lid and the familiar sound of Dr. Emily's slippers scuffing softly on the floor. Mandy joined her.

"Hello, dear," Dr. Emily greeted her. "You're up early."

"I didn't sleep very well," Mandy said, giving her mother a hug. "I think I might have upset Craig."

"Upset him? How?" Dr. Emily looked puzzled. She picked up Craig's abandoned glass, sniffed the soured milk, then poured it down the sink.

Mandy folded her arms and rested her back against the pantry door. She related the story Anna MacLeod had shared with her about Craig's ordeal with the snake and confessed how she had suddenly taken it into her head to confront Craig about his fears.

"I only want to be friends," Mandy ended miserably. "Now he's really angry."

Dr. Emily put an arm around Mandy's shoulders and pushed her tousled blond hair off her forehead. "I don't think so. I think he knows you'd like to include him. Behave as though nothing has happened. You've given him something to think about, and no harm has been done."

"Thanks, Mom." Mandy felt better as she realized there was nothing else she could do. She just hoped Craig didn't mind too much that she knew about his snake phobia.

"What are you and James going to do today?" Dr. Emily asked, changing the subject.

"We're going to go see Mrs. Stewart and ask her to give us some tips on how to make Ming even more perfect for the show." Mandy smiled. Thinking of Ming gave her a warm, happy feeling. She put Craig to the back of her mind and decided to go and wake James. There was Noodles to walk, too. It was going to be a busy day.

*   *   *

Mrs. Stewart was out in her garden, pruning a shrub into a smoothly rounded ball. She seemed pleased at the chance for a break from the hot morning sun.

"How's Kellogg?" Mandy asked.

"He's perked up a lot," she answered, pulling off her gardening gloves and tossing them onto a patio chair. "Nicole, on the other hand, is working far too hard and *still* hasn't come up with a suitable idea for her theme for Saturday. She's very frustrated."

"She must be," Mandy sympathized, noticing Gateau's portly frame gliding through the undergrowth. "There's Gateau, James. Look at his twitching tail!"

"I'm sure he thinks he's about to pounce on some unsuspecting prey." Mrs. Stewart laughed. "But it's very unlikely, at his age."

"We've come to ask you for some tips on grooming Ming for the show," James told her.

Mrs. Stewart smiled broadly. "Thomas has agreed? How wonderful!"

"Well," Mandy corrected her, "he agreed to let *us* enter and show Ming. So, you see, it's up to James and me."

"Well, I'll let you have Gateau's equipment. They're distantly related, so I'm sure he won't mind! You can take it over to Thomas's and begin getting Ming in shape right away," Mrs. Stewart said, her eyes shining. "How wonderful! Come with me."

James and Mandy followed Mrs. Stewart into the
house. On a shelf in the study was a sealed plastic box
marked GATEAU. She pried open the lid and began lifting
out a series of shiny gold medallions, curled glossy rib-
bons, and a collection of implements Mandy could not
name.

"Grooming a cat takes lots of patience," Mrs. Stewart
advised. "Some don't like it much; others love it. It just
depends on the cat."

Mandy spotted a framed photograph of Gateau on the
wall. There was no mistaking the proud expression on
his face. His smoothly muscular body was glowing with
good health, his chin was high and, in profile, he seemed
to be smiling.

"This is a bristle brush," Mrs. Stewart told them, holding out something that looked like a small body brush
used on horses. "It's used on short-haired cats to re-
move any loose, dead fur. And this is a wide-toothed
comb to take out any matted hair from the coat —
though if Ming has any, especially under her tummy,
you may be able to tease it out gently with your fingers. Don't forget to trim her nails if they're long.
The judges will look for good nails. This is the little clip-
per you'll need, but I expect your parents will help you
with that, Mandy. Also, a pair of nail scissors for tiny
clumps in the coat. Brush in the direction the hair

grows, and don't forget the belly and legs, OK?" she prompted.

"We won't," James said solemnly. "Thanks." He took the bag into which Mrs. Stewart had packed the grooming items.

"Yes, thank you," Mandy echoed, newly fired up by the pictures of Gateau and the thought of using the grooming kit on Ming. "We're going to do our best to remind people just how fantastic Appleheads are!"

From the doorway to Mr. Allardyce's shop, they heard him muttering. "Shoo, shoo, Noodles. I won't have you bothering Ming like this. Go find your own sunny spot, like a good boy."

"Hello, Mr. Allardyce," Mandy called.

The elderly man looked up from the window display area and waved. "Here's the cavalry to the rescue, just in time!" He smiled. "Noodles is being particularly bothersome today. He won't give Ming a minute's peace."

Mandy peered over a chest of drawers at Ming. She seemed determined to keep her spot in the window, still warm from the morning sun, but she was looking warily at Noodles, her blue eyes bright.

"Would she mind us practicing grooming her?" Mandy asked. "Mrs. Stewart has lent us Gateau's brushes and combs."

"I'll distract Noodles," James offered. "I can play with him while you tackle Ming."

Mandy looked at him gratefully. "Great, James. I'll try this, and then we can take Noodles for a walk on the beach."

"Pick her up, Mandy," Mr. Allardyce suggested. "She'd like a bit of attention. You can bring her to the back room. I have a table in there that should be just the right height for grooming her."

Mandy gently scooped Ming into her arms. The cat was as limp and soft as a toy, snuggling against Mandy's chest. Her triangular pink nose touched Mandy's chin, and she could feel Ming's soft breath on her cheek as she carried her.

"Here we are," said Thomas Allardyce, picking up a stack of magazines from the table. Mandy kissed Ming's silky head and lowered her onto the plastic tablecloth. She meowed and looked around with great interest. As each instrument was brought out of Mrs. Stewart's bag, Ming smelled it carefully and made a series of little noises ranging from a rumble to a delighted purr.

"I have a customer," Mr. Allardyce told Mandy as the doorbell rang in the shop, "so I'll leave you to it, OK?"

"That's fine, Mr. Allardyce," Mandy answered.

"Sit, Noodles!" she heard James command the dog. "Now, give me your paw!"

Mandy chuckled as she moved the grooming brush over Ming's fur. She could feel the ridge of the cat's delicate spine under the bristles and was careful not to press too hard.

"Does she like it?" James called, and Mandy half turned to see him lying on the floor, Noodles prancing around him like a great shaggy bear. "Er, I've given up with the dog training," he added sheepishly, pushing Noodles away as he tried to lick James's eyeglasses.

"She seems to," Mandy said, "judging by the purring!"

Ming stretched and turned, then rolled over and put her front paws onto the comb. With a skillful flick she sent it spinning onto the floor. When Mandy reached down to get it back, Ming sat up on the table and looked at her, a spark of mischief in her blue eyes. As Mandy began to straighten up, Ming reached and patted Mandy on the top of her head.

"You're a sweetie," Mandy told her, kissing her on the nose so that Ming gave a delicate sneeze. "You never put your claws out, do you?"

"What?" said James, adding, "Oh, Noodles! Don't do that!"

"Nothing." Mandy laughed. "Ming's being very good, that's all."

The Siamese cat lay on her side while Mandy ran the comb along her flank. Her coat was shining now, soft as silk, and Mandy felt pleased with her efforts. She looked around her, thinking that she could have stayed there with Ming forever. Above the table, up on the wall, was one of Thomas Allardyce's framed photographs of a basketful of kittens. Mandy counted eight of them peeping out over the rim, and the photographer had perfectly captured the curiosity and naughtiness of a kitten's expression. Hanging beside it was a watercolor painting of a ginger tabby cat on a wicker chair.

Beaumont is filled with cat lovers, Mandy thought as she picked the tiniest brush of all to do Ming's ears. Suddenly, she had an idea that made her heart leap, it was so good. Mr. Allardyce's collection of cat pictures would provide the perfect backdrop for the walls of Nicole's hotel! They would be an ideal talking point for the guests as they arrived. Mandy was so excited she almost called out to him, but he was busy at the other end of the shop with a customer and she thought better of it. Mr. Allardyce had already agreed to let them enter Ming in the show. Perhaps it would be better to talk to Nicole first and see what she thought.

"Mandy, Noodles is getting restless," James announced, coming up behind her. He was out of breath, and his glasses were at an angle. "I think I'd better take him out."

"I'm just about finished with Ming," Mandy said. "She's drowsy from the brushing. I'll put her back in the window and come with you."

Noodles seemed thrilled to be going for a walk. He stepped along proudly, not tugging quite so hard at his leash. He was putting more pressure on the injured foot and had almost succeeded in shredding the grubby bandage with his teeth. As they passed the door to Mrs. Gibb's shop, James waved.

Mrs. Gibb waved back, smiling, and called out, "Thanks so much!"

Mandy told James about her idea for Nicole's hotel display. "There must be eighty pictures, if not more," she said. "Wouldn't it be terrific?"

"It would," James acknowledged, "but d'you think Mr. Allardyce would agree? They're his pride and joy, those pictures."

"Well, no harm would come to them," Mandy reasoned. "I don't see why not."

"Look!" James pointed and stopped short. "There's Nicole now. Why don't we ask her?"

Nicole was hurrying toward them, looking harassed. She was carrying a large cardboard box.

"Nicole!" Mandy caught her attention.

"Hi, James, Mandy," she said. "Whew! Isn't it hot?"

"We're taking Noodles to the beach," said James.

"Have a dip for me," said Nicole, sounding envious. "I've got to get back to the hotel." She lifted the box. "These are new wine glasses. We ran out."

"Wait," Mandy pleaded as Nicole stepped around them. "We have an idea for your welcome theme. We think it might be really good."

Nicole shifted the box to her hip. "OK, what's your idea?"

"Have you seen Mr. Allardyce's cats?" James began.

Nicole looked surprised. "You mean Ming?"

"No, no!" Mandy smiled. "His cat art — his pictures. He's got tons of great pictures, drawings, and paintings of cats everywhere!"

"In the shop?" Nicole cocked her head, seeming more and more interested.

"Yes, all over the walls. If you asked him, I'm sure he'd lend them to you," Mandy finished, crossing her arms in triumph.

"How many are there?" Nicole took off her sunglasses with her free hand. "Enough to cover the lobby and the dining room?"

"I'm sure," Mandy said.

"That's fantastic!" Nicole grinned. "I'll talk to my manager. Now I'd better hurry back to work."

Nicole set out at a brisk pace, her high-heeled sandals tip-tapping on the pavement. "You might have saved the day!" she called back over her shoulder.

Mandy's spirits were high as they crossed the road and ran down the steps to the beach. She felt positive that Ming would make a great impression at the show, and now it looked as though they had helped Nicole, too.

They took off their shoes, and James let Noodles off the leash. He barked joyfully, turning in circles to show his appreciation, then blundered into an abandoned sand castle. They started running across the burning sand toward the water, dodging the brightly colored beach umbrellas. The dog bounded into the water, allowing the waves to swirl around him, cooling his tummy.

"Oh, that's nice," said James when the water splashed up around his knees. "Let's spend the rest of the day right here."

Mandy nodded and fished in the pocket of her shorts for a couple of coins. "I even have enough money for ice cream," she declared happily.

Noodles was exhausted by the time they came back up from the beach. His pink tongue lolled as he walked sedately at James's side. As soon as they reached Mrs. Gibb's back door, he went straight into his basket and collapsed with a big sigh.

"This is for you," said Mrs. Gibb, holding out a large, sticky chocolate cake. "I made it to say thank you to you both."

"Oh! What a fantastic-looking cake!" Mandy said.

"Yum!" James's eyes lit up. "Thanks!"

Mandy and James gave Noodles a farewell pat and carried the cake back to the clinic. As they opened the door to the house, Mandy felt a pang of worry. She wondered if Craig would still be angry with her.

"What do you have there?" asked Dr. Adam when they came in.

Mandy set the cake down. "A present from Mrs. Gibb for walking Noodles," she said.

"How nice!" Dr. Emily smiled. "Anyone like a piece for a snack?"

"Yes, please!" James said quickly.

"I've got good news," said Dr. Adam. "Mrs. Sullivan called a little while ago to say that Katie the calf is much better and eating normally."

"Oh, good!" Mandy said.

"Now, tell us all about your day," Dr. Adam prompted as he found a suitable knife to the cut the cake.

"Yes," Mandy's mother agreed. "But first, Mandy, would you take some cake up to Craig? I'm sure he'd like a piece. He's in his room."

Mandy's heart sank. She felt really nervous after their quarrel the night before, but she knew she had to make an effort. "OK," she said, and caught James's eye. He raised his eyebrows at her.

Mandy carried the small plate up the stairs to the top of the house. There was music coming from inside Craig's room, so she knocked hard on the door. It opened, and Craig looked out at her, his face expressionless.

"For you," Mandy said, trying to muster a smile.

Craig's eyes fell on the deliciously gooey dark chocolate cake. "I'm not hungry, thank you," he said, and firmly shut the door.

Mandy's shoulders slumped. She turned and trudged down the stairs. "I give up," she said to herself. "I just give up!"

There was little sign of Craig over the next two days. Mandy couldn't help feeling relieved, but she was still worried about him. He was such a loner! Her mom tried to reassure her when Mandy told her about her concern.

"He's fine," Dr. Emily said. "He seems really busy with his soccer practice. I'm sure he's OK, dear. He just prefers his own company."

Mandy and James had soon found that they were as busy with the routine on Jersey as they were back home in Welford. They helped in the clinic and the residential unit, walked Noodles, played with Ming — and spent time on the beach. Eventually, Mandy had to admit that it was hard to worry too much about Craig when they were having such a good time.

Nicole had been to see Thomas Allardyce, and he had readily agreed to allow his collection to hang in the hotel foyer on the day of the show. When Nicole called Mandy to thank her, she sounded thrilled.

"It's a great idea, really super, Mandy," she enthused. "They're going to look just right."

"I'm so pleased," Mandy said happily. "We'll definitely come and see them when they're hanging in the hotel."

"Have you and James had a cream tea yet?" Nicole asked suddenly.

"Yes, but we wouldn't mind another!" Mandy said. "Why?"

"I want to say thank you," Nicole explained. "Come and have a cream tea at my house tomorrow — say, four o'clock?"

"Thanks!" Mandy said, winking at James, who was hovering near the phone, trying to listen in.

"I'll invite Mr. Allardyce, and why don't you bring your parents — and Craig?" Nicole added. "We can have a pre–cat show party!"

"Um, OK, thank you," Mandy said. "We'll see you tomorrow." She replaced the receiver.

"Not Mrs. MacLeod?" James groaned.

"No, Nicole Stewart," Mandy grinned. "We're going to a pre–cat show cream tea."

"Hooray!" said James.

On Thursday morning during breakfast, Mandy's mother managed to persuade Craig that he should go with them to the Stewarts' for tea. He seemed reluctant, and when it was time to leave, he walked a pace or two behind the others as they made their way to the house.

"Thank heavens for Jennifer," said Dr. Adam, fanning his face with a straw hat. "It's too hot to be in the clinic today."

"Yes," Dr. Emily agreed. "But we have no appointments, so it should be peaceful enough. She'll call us if there's an emergency."

Mrs. Stewart and Nicole had set up a table under the awning on the patio. Thomas Allardyce was busy gathering chairs and placing them in a circle. A small breeze stirred the edges of a pretty cloth, and James's eyes bulged when he saw a towering pile of scones, still steaming from the oven.

"Wow!" said Mandy. "This looks amazing."

"There's clotted cream ice cream a bit later, if you've got room," Mrs. Stewart said as they took their seats.

Gateau was lying in the shade of a chair, stretched out to his fullest on the cool flagstone patio.

"Ming is indoors," said Thomas Allardyce. "She's not a great one for the heat."

"Do cats suffer in the heat?" James asked. "I mean, they don't sweat, do they?"

"You're right, James," said Mrs. Stewart. "Dogs perspire by panting, but cats can't perspire at all. So they keep cool by doing very little on hot days. They lie around in the coolest places they can find."

"That reminds me," Mr. Allardyce said, passing around the plate of scones. "I delivered the last box of cat pictures to your hotel this morning, Nicole."

"Oh, thank you!" said Nicole. "It's going to look so great when they're all hung on the walls — just like an art gallery dedicated to cats!"

"I like the picture of the Victorian lady wheeling her cat in a pram," said James, taking the bowl of strawberry jam Mrs. Stewart offered him.

"Me, too," said Mandy. Then she frowned. She had heard a faint but distinctive cry. "What's that?" It might have been a child, or a gull.

"What's what?" asked James.

"Shh!" Mandy urged him, holding up her hand. Everyone stared at her. There it was again, a long, high whine that ended on a desperate note. Mandy strained to make sense of it, but her heart had begun a dull, fearful thudding. She heard the cry for a third time, this time sounding even more urgent. It was a sound she recognized with sudden, heart-stopping clarity.

"That's Ming!" she cried. "I know it is. Something's wrong!"

Mandy's chair thudded to the ground as she rushed

away from the table. She was down the steps of the patio and across the yard in a second and racing to wrench open the gate that led to the lane that ran behind the row of houses. She narrowly avoided a boy on a bicycle. He wobbled dangerously as she burst out and ran toward Mr. Allardyce's shop.

To her horror, she saw thin dark gray plumes of smoke coiling from the cracks of the back door of Allardyce Antiques.

"Fire!" Mandy shouted as loudly as she could. "Help! Fire!"

Nine

The smoke seeping around the door thickened as Mandy watched helplessly. She grabbed the handle of the locked door and rattled it, listening in dismay to the repeated yowling of the Siamese inside.

"Ming!" Mandy peered through the kitchen window of the burning shop. "Oh, please be safe, Ming." With her nose pressed against the glass and her trembling hands cupped around her face, she could see bright orange flames and billowing smoke. There was no sign of Ming.

Mandy frantically looked left and right, wondering if she should try to break the window. But then she heard footsteps on the path behind her and turned to see Thomas Allardyce with a big bunch of keys.

"The fire engine is on its way," shouted James, racing past in the lane. "I'll go warn Mrs. Gibb."

Mandy saw her parents running toward the clinic. "We're going to evacuate the residential unit it case it spreads," Dr. Adam called.

"I'll give you a hand," Mrs. Stewart shouted, and began to run to catch up. "Nicole's gone to the house on the other side."

Mr. Allardyce looked down at Mandy. "It looks like it's just you and me here," he said. He unlocked the door and pushed it open, putting out an arm to keep Mandy back. Mandy was far too sensible to risk running into the shop; what she wanted was an escape route for Ming!

From among the clutter on the floor, amid the swirl of smoke and the crackle of the flames, a small dark face appeared, wide-eyed with terror. Ming gave a piteous wail and slunk toward safety. As she dashed out the door, Mandy bent down and gathered her up in her arms.

"Ming! Oh, Ming, you're all right!" she said, burying her face in the cat's smoke-stained coat. Ming's body was tense with fright, but as Mandy soothed her, she began to relax. Ming sneezed once, then again, and pushed herself higher until her nose was touching

Mandy's ear. Mandy's hair covered the cat's face like a curtain. The cat's breathing was rapid and warm, and it tickled Mandy's neck. Ming snuggled there, finding comfort in a place where she could no longer smell the acrid smoke. Mandy marveled that, frightened though she was, Ming hadn't once used her claws to cling on.

When Thomas Allardyce had made certain that his beloved cat was safe, he made a grab for the fire extinguisher hanging above the stovetop and went into his shop. Mandy gave a sigh of relief as she heard the first faint wail of a fire engine heading their way. She decided to take Ming to Mrs. Stewart's house. It was very close, and seeing Gateau might help Ming calm down.

"Come on," she said softly. "I'm going to get you away from all this noise and confusion, poor girl."

Mandy wondered if the cat would panic when she began walking down the road. She could hear the fire engine pulling up on the main street, its alarm wailing. But Ming stayed exactly where she was, hiding under Mandy's hair, her front paws warm around Mandy's neck. When they reached Mrs. Stewart's back door, she peeped out to see where she was and gave a third, delicate sneeze.

"You've inhaled a little smoke," Mandy told Ming, reaching out to open the door. But someone was already there. The door flew open, so hard that Mandy had to jump back to avoid colliding with it. Craig bolted

out the door just as Mrs. Stewart and Mandy's mother came in through the gate from the lane.

"Goodness!" said Mrs. Stewart, stopping short with surprise. "Are you all right, Craig?"

There was a sudden silence. Craig stood there, shifting unhappily from foot to foot. His arms were straight out in front of him, rigid, a heavy black-and-orange loop coiled around one wrist. Mandy felt her mouth drop open in astonishment when she realized what he was carrying. Craig was holding the corn snake! Kellogg's head swayed from side to side in alarmed confusion, his split tongue going like crazy. Even to Mandy, the corn snake's posture appeared a little menacing. How must he appear to a boy who was petrified of snakes?

"Take him!" Craig begged as Nicole suddenly arrived in the garden. She was panting for breath, her eyes wide with concern, and Mandy saw that the heel of one of her shoes was broken.

"Kellogg!" Nicole whispered, and took the snake as Craig thrust him at her. He had to shake his wrist free of the tail end.

"Quick! I'm going back in for the cat. I saw him in the kitchen!" he said at once.

"Gateau?" said Mrs. Stewart, puzzled.

Dr. Emily put her hand on Craig's arm. "It's all right, Craig," she said quietly. "The fire is under control. It won't spread to Mrs. Stewart's house. You can leave Gateau where he is."

Craig flushed. "Oh, OK," he said.

Mandy was so surprised by what Craig had done that she didn't know what to say. What incredible courage he had shown, dashing in to rescue the animals from the fire he had thought was about to spread into their home! Mandy could hardly believe it. She wanted to give him a hug to thank him, but she was too shy. Besides, Craig was still looking angry.

"Look out!" Everyone turned as the shout echoed down the lane. Mandy recognized James's voice, and in spite of everything, she began to smile.

"Stop!" James yelled weakly, coming into view in the lane. "Do as you're told!"

Noodles came bouncing through the gate, his tongue lolling and his ears flapping up and down. James was seconds behind, looking defeated and very hot.

"He slipped out of his leash," he explained sheepishly. "Mrs. Gibb wasn't there, so I took him, only he got loose."

Dr. Emily was trying not to laugh. She put her arm around James's shoulders. Noodles greeted everyone in turn, then hurried over to inspect the only person he didn't know well — Craig. The dog put his nose into Craig's palm and sniffed it with great interest. Mandy held her breath, wondering what Craig would do. As she watched, he put a hesitant hand on Noodles's head. Noodles sat down, pressing up close against Craig's legs, and looked up at him with warm, loving eyes.

Mandy's eyes filled with sudden tears. She blinked them away. "You're a hero," she said simply, smiling at Craig. "Even Noodles knows that."

"Not me," he replied, his fingers playing with Noodles's curly coat. "*You*, maybe. I saw you trying to get into the burning shop. You'd do anything to save the life of an animal."

For an instant, Mandy wondered if Craig was making fun of her, but when she looked at him, she saw that he was looking directly back at her and that his eyes were twinkling in a kind way.

"Yes, good job, Craig!" said Mrs. Stewart.

"Thanks for rescuing Kellogg!" Nicole put in.

"*You* rescued the snake?" asked James, looking from Craig to Mandy. When Mandy nodded, James's eyebrows shot up.

"Well, not really. When Mandy took off, all of you rushed next door," Craig explained, shrugging. "I thought the fire might come this way and that I'd better get the pets out. I found the snake in that glass case, but it looked too heavy to carry, so I just took him out. I hope that's OK?" he added nervously.

"Absolutely! A courageous decision," said Mrs. Stewart. "Now, let's all go inside and settle the animals down. Then we'll go back and see if Thomas needs our help."

"Good idea," Mandy said. Ming still lay sleepily against her shoulder, her blue eyes half closed. Mandy loved her fiercely. She felt very proud that Ming had been the one to raise the alarm in the first place.

"I think that Siamese cat deserves a special thank-you," said Craig as he went into the house behind her.

"Ming," Mandy said, turning and smiling. "Her name is Ming."

"Ming," Craig corrected himself. "She's a smart cat, that's for sure."

"I agree," Mandy grinned. "A very smart — and — beautiful — cat!"

They hadn't been crowded into Mrs. Stewart's living room for long when Dr. Adam and Thomas Allardyce appeared.

"Thomas!" Mrs. Stewart gasped, hugging her friend. "We're so sorry for you. Is there much damage?"

Mr. Allardyce looked very weary. The pocket of his shirt had been ripped, and he had a black smudge across his forehead. He shook his head. "Not much, Deborah," he replied, gratefully accepting a chair. "The firefighters are dealing with it now, and it's well under control."

"What happened?" Nicole asked.

"It seems the sun is to blame," said Dr. Adam, rubbing his cheek and leaving a sooty black mark. "The fire was started by sunshine hitting the lens of a magnifying glass lying in the window! It's a good thing Thomas wasn't very far away or the whole shop might have gone up."

"Thank you, Mandy," said Mr. Allardyce. "If you hadn't heard Ming call out . . ." His voice shook and trailed off.

"We should thank Ming," Mandy said, putting out her hand to the Siamese who was curled up on a cushion on the sofa. Ming gave a little rumble in acknowledgment.

"You know, that windowsill has been a little unlucky all around," Mr. Allardyce said, recovering himself. "Nothing but trouble!" He glared playfully at Noodles, who was sitting beside Craig. The dog looked up and fixed Mr. Allardyce with a beady eye, then wagged his stumpy tail.

"You'll have to make a temporary place for Ming in the shop while the windowsill is rebuilt," Mandy suggested. "Somewhere Noodles can't reach!"

"Good idea," Mr. Allardyce agreed. "Though it will have to be a spot in the sun."

"I'm very glad there's no serious damage to anything or anyone," said Nicole, reaching out to pet Gateau as he stalked past. Mandy thought that the elderly cat looked a bit put out by all the upheaval around him.

"And it's a good thing that Mr. Allardyce's cat pictures weren't still hanging inside the shop," Mandy remarked.

"Goodness, yes," said Mrs. Stewart. "The smoke would have ruined them."

There was a knock on the front door, and Nicole got up to open it. Sarah Jane Gibb stood there, looking flustered.

"Is everybody all right?" she asked anxiously. "Noodles . . . ?"

"Everybody's fine," Nicole assured her, stepping aside to let her in. "James went to get Noodles the moment the fire started."

"Oh, thank you!" Mrs. Gibb looked around at the gathering in the sitting room. Noodles hurried over to jump up and lick her face. "It seems I'm never around when I'm needed! I'd gone out to do a bit of shopping. I'm so sorry about the shop, Thomas."

"No real harm done, Sarah Jane," said Mr. Allardyce.

"Sit down," Mrs. Stewart urged her. "I'll get the rest of that cream tea we began, and we'll tell you all about it!"

Ten

When Mandy woke up on Saturday morning, it was clear and bright and much cooler than before. She noticed the change in temperature right away and felt glad. She wanted Ming to be as comfortable as possible on her big day. In spite of the fire, the Siamese was looking in peak condition, and Mandy's mom had pronounced her completely fit. Excitement fluttered through Mandy as she dressed. It would be wonderful if Ming won a prize!

In the kitchen, her dad and James were starting to eat a stack of pancakes. To Mandy's surprise, Craig was sitting at the table, too, dribbling honey from a spoon onto his pancakes.

"Hi," Mandy said casually, acting as though Craig joined them for breakfast every day. He gave her a quick smile as she sat down. Dr. Emily delivered a pancake to her plate with a small plop.

"Dad and I have a patient to see," she said. "We won't be long. We plan to leave for the show around lunchtime, OK?"

Mandy nodded. "James and I will pick up Ming and have her ready by then."

"Mrs. Stewart is going to help us," James added.

"Good. We'll see you later." Dr. Adam plunged the griddle into a basin of cold water with a sizzle and followed Mandy's mom out of the room.

When they'd gone, Mandy felt a little shyness creep over her again. But to her surprise, Craig seemed far more relaxed.

"My dad called this morning," he said. "I told him about the fire — and Kellogg."

"What did he say?" Mandy asked.

Craig glanced down at his half-eaten pancake. "He couldn't believe I'd handled that snake! I guess he was pleased, though."

"I bet he was," James commented.

"I'm sorry I've been such a pain," Craig said suddenly, looking up again. "Ever since I ended up in the hospital after that snakebite, I've tried my best to keep away from animals. But somehow, on Thursday, it was different."

"How?" asked James, frowning.

"I don't know, really." Craig ran his fingers through his curly hair. "I was so focused on trying to save lives during that fire I didn't stop to think that I might be putting myself in danger. I just did it."

"It must be hard," Mandy said sympathetically. "I mean, I've grown up with animals and I love them, but I know not everyone feels the same way."

Craig shot her a grateful look. "You're right," he agreed. "Leaving Scotland and saying good-bye to my friends, my school, and my soccer team was really difficult. I guess I was pretty resentful."

"Do you think you'll feel differently from now on?" James prompted.

"Differently?" Craig thought for a moment. "Well, probably not, but maybe it'll be easier to be around the animals that come into the clinic. I mean, I've kind of proved to myself that I can handle snakes and dogs, so I guess I can cope with anything!"

"Animals can sense fear in people," Mandy pointed out. "They seem to know when people are not comfortable with them and don't trust them."

Craig laughed. "Well, I *didn't* trust Kellogg not to bite me when I grabbed him out of that tank!"

"That makes you even more brave," Mandy said.

"Yes, really," James said admiringly. He added, "Corn snakes don't bite, you know."

Mandy finished her pancake. "James and I have to go get Ming ready for the show. Are you coming?"

"No," Craig said, taking his plate to the sink. "I have a soccer game." He turned and grinned at them. "But I'll be there to congratulate Ming when you get back."

"Cross your fingers," Mandy said, grinning.

"Good luck," Craig called as they went into the hall.

James nudged Mandy and gave her a thumbs-up sign. She smiled broadly at him. It looked like Craig was going to be OK after all.

"Right here," said Mrs. Stewart, turning Ming so that Mandy could clip away an uneven bit of her coat. "And look, there's a tiny mat of fur between those toes."

Mandy was concentrating hard, wielding the small scissors very carefully so as not to stab Ming with their sharp points. The Siamese was lying on her side on the table in Mr. Allardyce's back room, purring loudly. Every so often she raised her leg and began doing her own grooming. Mandy could hear the rasping of her rough tongue on her coat.

"Now for her ears," Mr. Allardyce urged, leaning over to have a look at his cat. "They should be pink and clean." There were no customers in the shop, so he had come to watch the preparations for the show.

"Are her eyes clear?" James asked. "What do you think, Mrs. Stewart?"

"Clear as crystal, blue as the sky. Perfect!" she replied.

"Thank goodness," Mandy said. "After the lamp oil and the smoke from the fire, it's a wonder she's presentable at all!"

"She's more than presentable," Mrs. Stewart declared, planting a kiss on Ming's smooth head. "She looks like a champion to me!"

Ming yawned as though tired of all the attention, then rolled over onto her back and stretched. Suddenly, she jumped up and butted her head against Mandy's cheek, purring hard.

"I hope so," Mandy whispered. "Oh, I hope so."

Ming traveled to the show in a small wire cage padded with a blue blanket. She protested loudly all the way there, sitting on the backseat of the Land Rover between James and Mandy.

"What a fuss!" Dr. Adam grumbled, winking at Mandy in the rearview mirror. "Don't look so concerned, Mandy," he added. "Most cats make a terrible racket in vehicles."

"She's fine, Mandy," her mother assured her. "She's just unused to the motion."

The trip to the agricultural center was a short one, and soon they were pulling into a parking area already jam-packed with cars, trucks, and trailers. A huge yellow banner flapped in a cooling breeze from the top of the massive building, proclaiming this the GOVERNING COUNCIL OF THE CAT FANCY SHOW.

"Phew!" said James. "How many people own cats on this island?"

"People travel far and wide to get to shows like this one," Dr. Emily explained. "This gives breeders a chance to see how their own cats match up to the animals of fellow breeders."

"It's also a fun day out for cat owners who just want to enjoy their cats," said Dr. Adam.

Mandy lifted Ming out. The cage was fairly heavy, but she tried not to swing the Siamese as she walked along. Inside the vast hall, Dr. Emily shook hands with several of the organizers and introduced Mandy, Ming, and James. Then she took her place behind a long plastic-topped table and began to set out the instruments she would need for checking the cats.

Mandy joined a line of people waiting with their animals to see the vet. Each cat had to pass a simple veterinary inspection before it was allowed to take part in the show. The noise in the hall was deafening, the buzz of voices competing with the meows of what seemed like a thousand or more cats. James put his hands over his ears, but Ming, Mandy noticed, didn't seem to mind. She was content now that she was out of the car, and sat on her blanket looking around with great curiosity. Mandy put her ear to the cage and heard Ming purring away happily to herself.

All around the hall, banners announced different breeds. Each group had its own judge, and Mandy looked around for where they would be taking Ming.

"Adolescents," she read. "Maiden, Debutante, Senior. Gosh, where do we go?"

"Over there." Dr. Adam pointed helpfully as he came up behind them. "See the sign that says Novice? That's you."

A steward handed Mandy a tag with a number on it and a vetting-in slip. She shuffled along with Ming in the cage until she reached the third vet in the line, an important-looking man in a white coat. As she stopped in front of him, she caught her mother's eye and smiled. The vet took Mandy's form, then lifted Ming out and quickly checked her skin for signs of ringworm. Her nose was dry and clear, her eyes bright.

"She's in peak condition," he said, and smiled, putting Ming back in. "Good luck, young lady. Next!"

"Thank you," Mandy mumbled, suddenly over-whelmed by nervousness. What did she have to do now? She looked around for her mother, but Dr. Emily Hope was examining a long-haired cat with a blunt, typically Persian face and didn't see her.

"Look," James said. "We're being called to the middle of the room."

In the center of the high-roofed, echoing building, a long row of tables held a series of identical cages. There were already cats inside some of them, yowling in frustration. Mandy was told by a steward to put Ming into a cage at the end of the line. The number on the wire mesh matched the one she had on her tag. There was a bowl of water in the cage and some bedding. Mandy knew she would have to leave Ming alone for the judging, so she put her finger through the mesh and scratched Ming's head in farewell. Ming didn't seem comfortable as Mandy turned to go. She stuck her slender paw through the wire and tried to catch her hand as she left.

"I won't be far away," Mandy whispered. "Be a good girl. I love you."

Mandy and her dad joined James amid a crush of eager spectators at one side of the hall. Mandy had to stand on tiptoe to see the judges moving slowly down the line of cats. Her heart was pounding so hard it made her dizzy.

"How's it going?"

Mandy spun around to find Craig and Sarah Jane Gibb beside her.

"Oh, hi! I'm so nervous. Ming's over there on the table. The judges are coming to her now," Mandy told them in a rush.

"I thought you were playing soccer," James said to Craig.

"Game's over," Craig replied. "Mrs. Gibb gave me a lift. I wanted to see how Ming was doing."

Mandy smiled at him. "Thanks."

"She's going to be perfect," Mrs. Gibb said. Her blond hair had been done up into a French braid, but in the bustle of the hall it had come loose, and her plump cheeks were flushed with heat.

"I hope you didn't bring Noodles," James said, grinning at her. "Imagine that dog in here with all these cats!"

"No, he's at home," said Mrs. Gibb. "Craig told me that tomorrow is your last day on the island. Noodles is really going to miss you both!"

"Er, I could try walking him, if you like," Craig offered hesitantly.

As much as she was straining to keep an eye on Ming, Mandy turned and looked at him in surprise.

"Craig!" said Sarah Jane Gibb, clearly surprised. "Really? *You?*"

"I'll have a try," Craig repeated. "I like him. He's funny — and he seems to have taken a shine to me."

"Well, thank you," Mrs. Gibb said warmly. "That would be a huge favor."

"Noodles might be the start of a whole new career, Craig!" Mandy teased.

"Don't worry," Craig shot back, his eyes twinkling. "I'm not going to be giving up soccer practice to clean out animal cages or anything — not like some people I know!"

"Shhhh!" James urged them. "Ming's being taken out of her cage."

All eyes were on the Siamese as she was carried across to the judges' table. In the bright lighting of the hall, her coat gleamed. Her four dark paws and her round chocolate-colored cheeks were a wonderful contrast to her pale body.

"Little ghost of a tiger," Mandy said under her breath.

On the table, Ming lifted her pretty face to the judge. Just to the left, Mandy noticed that a beautiful silver Wedgehead Siamese was being examined. Could Ming win over this sleek and imperious creature?

Then she saw a large Applehead in the arms of a woman who was beaming with pride as she placed that cat on the table in front of the judges.

Mandy nudged James. "Look, another Applehead!" she whispered. "But not nearly as beautiful as Ming."

"It's good to see another Applehead," said James.

Mandy could hardly breathe as cats were brought from their holding cages and paraded in front of the judges. The Wedgeheads had such a distinctive look, but none of them had the charm of Ming, in Mandy's opinion.

She held her breath while Ming was being carefully examined, but it was all over very quickly — and then a steward picked Ming up and carried her back to her cage.

It seemed to Mandy that hours passed while more cats were brought forward and taken back. The room became a blur of white coats and beautiful animals.

"It doesn't matter," Mandy said to James, after another Applehead had made an appearance. Clearly, they had a loyal following on the island. Mandy wondered briefly if they were all related to Gateau! "It really doesn't matter if she doesn't win a prize. After all . . ."

James put a finger to his lips to shush her. His eyes were riveted on the judges as, at last, a metallic announcement rang out from a PA system that echoed around the building.

"In the Oriental category, Novice class . . ."

"This is it!" Sarah Jane Gibbs whispered, clutching at Mandy's sleeve. Mandy looked over to where her mother was standing and waved. Dr. Adam slipped an arm around Mandy's shoulders. He was straining forward, frowning in concentration.

"Best of breed award goes to . . ."

Mandy squeezed her eyes shut.

"Sud Su Ming, an eighteen-month-old Applehead owned by Mr. Thomas Allardyce of Beaumont, Jersey."

Mandy felt her heart do a somersault as applause erupted around the room. Dr. Adam let out a whoop of triumph, and Mandy's mom came hurrying over. Mandy was enveloped in hugs from all sides.

"Congratulations! Good job! You worked so hard!"

"Thomas will be thrilled!"

"So will Mrs. Stewart!"

"Thank you," Mandy said, wondering how quickly she would be able to see Ming. She edged forward, trying to get a glimpse of the Siamese. Suddenly, the crowd began to stream forward to gather up their animals, and Dr. Emily eased Mandy along into the middle of the room.

Ming was sitting in her cage on the table, gazing about her in fascination. A bright blue rosette and medallion had been pinned to one side and a blue winner's certificate was attached to the wire, fluttering temptingly in the breeze from the overhead fans. Ming put out a paw and tried to catch it through the mesh.

"Ming!" Mandy said, opening the lid and reaching in to pick her up. The Siamese greeted her noisily, making a kind of mewling and rumbling sound as Mandy kissed her face. Ming put her two soft front paws on Mandy's cheeks and touched her nose to Mandy's chin.

"You won," she told Ming. "You won for the Appleheads! You beat the Wedgeheads!"

Ming didn't seem interested. Instead, she took a swipe at the glinting gold medallion and sent it clattering to the floor.

Mandy laughed and hugged the beautiful cat tighter as people began to gather around: Craig and Sarah Jane Gibb, Jennifer and James, all smiling and reaching out to pet the adorable little Siamese. Mandy was thrilled that Ming had won, but all the medallions and rosettes in the world were not as important to her as the friends she'd made in Beaumont — people, as well as animals!